Clay backed her up against the tiled wall, pressing his body against hers. He parted her thighs with a sideways brush of his leg and stood between them, the throb of his sex vibrating between her heat.

"I want you, Dee…so…much," he uttered in a ragged whisper, rocking his hips against her.

She arched her neck as the water poured over them, the one element that kept the temperature from skyrocketing out of control.

"I'm not afraid. Not anymore. Just unsure of my…responses. Oh, Clay," she whimpered when he slid a finger along the sensitive bud and rubbed. Her legs began to tremble, "I don't know…if I will…can satis—"

"Sssh. Don't." He cupped her breasts, took one, then the other into his mouth. "Just let it happen." He turned off the water and scooped her up into his arms, covering her lips with his. "There's nothing to compare this with."

He carried her into the bedroom and laid her on the bed, momentarily standing over her, taking in the raw beauty before him. "We're going to create a new beginning."

QUIET STORM

DONNA HILL

Genesis Press, Inc.

Indigo Love Stories

An imprint of Genesis Press, Inc.
Publishing Company

Genesis Press, Inc.
P.O. Box 101
Columbus, MS 39703

ISBN-13: 978-1-58571-226-7
ISBN-10: 1-58571-226-4
Manufactured in the United States of America

First Edition 1998
Second Edition 2007

Visit us at www.genesis-press.com or call at 1-888-Indigo-1

ACKNOWLEDGEMENTS

As always, to Gregg who continues to inspire, support, and encourage me in all that I do. And to his favorite phrase, which has become my battle cry: Why don't you try something different?" Thanks babe! To my dear friend Gwynne Forster, whose love and support, keen writer's eye, dry wit and cheerleader spirit keep me going...and humble. Thanks, sweetie. To Panic Steele-Perkins, my agent and my friend. Panic, thank you for all of your support, advice, and eye-to-the-sky philosophy I believe '98 is our year!!

CHAPTER I

"She's dead," one woman said to the other as she took a sip from her flute of champagne. "The award will be given posthumously." She waved a hand dismissively as if she were discussing the weather.

"You are so crude," her friend replied, a sagacious grin framing her wide mouth. "Just because the woman hasn't been seen in years doesn't mean she's dead."

"She might as well be. What has she done lately?"

"I don't know, some kind of Foundation thing or whatever. Anyway, you're still angry because she landed Cord Herrera and you didn't. Get over it. That was years ago and he's moved on. So should you. He's a gigolo anyway."

"Humph, that's not the point."

Deanna Winters and her friend, and business associate, Tracy Moore stood nearby with their backs turned to the two experts at character assassination.

"Come on Dee, you don't need to listen to this."

Deanna forced a smile. "No, but they need to listen to this."

She turned toward the direction of the voices, and leaned a bit closer. "I'm not dead. But don't tell anyone." She heard gasps. "And by the way, Cord Herrera was incredible." That part was up for discussion, but they didn't need to know. "Have a nice evening, ladies."

"Deanna Winters you...are...awful." Tracy laughed. "And I love it. I wish you could have seen their stupid little overly made-up faces!"

"So do I," she said. "But I can just imagine." The two friends giggled as they wended their way through the mass of humanity.

During intermission, the star-studded crowd continued to mill about the huge lobby of Radio City Music Hall, flaunting smiles, lots of leg and cleavage, seeing who they could see and being assured that they would be seen. Glittering gowns and diamonds competed on equal footing with the steady flash of camera bulbs.

Deanna moved anonymously through the throng, a steady smile etched on her face. Her hand securely clasped Tracy's elbow as they glided around the knots of people. She knew the milieu well. Her years beneath the spotlight and in the limelight were forever embedded in her memory.

At times she missed it. She missed the exhilarating rush of adrenaline when she stepped out onto the stage: when her fingers stroked the keys, captured every note, every nuance, and took it to another level: when she expertly transported the audience on a musical odyssey that jolted them to their feet, brought roars of "more" until they were exhausted from the heat of adulation. There was no feeling like it. Her personal happiness was only experienced during those brief moments. Still, she had found a way around and through it. She found a way to use what she had for so much more than a single hour of pleasure. Or maybe she should say: A way had been made.

The lobby lights began to flicker, signaling the end of intermission. The crowd moved like a slow tide heading for the shore of their seats. The rise and fall of voices washed over the historic edifice, punctuated by twittering laughter and deep guffaws.

At that precise moment, almost as if the sea of people had parted at his command—like a '90s version of Moses in *The Ten Commandments*—Cord Herrera swaggered through the doors of Radio City Music Hall. Flashbulbs instantly went off in a frenzy of white-hot light, as if they'd been programmed to record his every movement. In his blue-black Armani tuxedo, accented by diamond cufflinks, a white collarless shirt—and just enough shadow on his hard jaw to give him a rugged appearance—Cord looked every bit the star he'd become.

Heads turned. Several women, even some men, stopped to gape and admire the heartthrob of more than a dozen mega-movie hits. Others moved on, wrapped in their own cape of self-importance. Cord smiled and waved, whispering a word here, an anecdote there, and posed for the cameras as he made his way to his reserved seat. His partner for the evening, a stunning blonde, clung possessively to his arm, reveling in the overflow of homage that spilled her way.

Cord entered the amphitheater, acknowledging the recognition from his colleagues with practiced tilts of his chin. But his thoughts were centered on the woman who sat three rows ahead of him.

"I have an Oscar...two Oscars," Cord whispered into the ear of his companion. "Supported numerous causes to which I've lent my name, provided credibility, raised money. I held little black babies in Africa. So you tell me, why am I, Cord Herrera, not on that stage being honored tonight?"

Cord's companion listened quietly, monitoring his level of discontent and observing the people seated around them. The women who drank him in with hungry gazes. Women who wished they were in her place. But if only they knew.

Women were always drawn to him. In Argentina, the youngest male child with six sisters, Cordero Rodriquez Herrera wanted for nothing. Suckled and pampered his entire life, Cord only knew how to receive, without learning the art of giving. He'd been ignored by his father, whose love and affection Cord struggled to attain. So he sought it from everyone around him. For Cord, anything less than absolute devotion was intolerable.

Cord's agitation caught the discreet corner-of-the-eye looks. Nevertheless, his frustration level continued to escalate.

"I tell you, when I first met Deanna, yes, she was at the top of the charts, commercials, endorsements. She was *People* magazine's Woman of the Year. Everyone loved Deanna."

His companion put a finger over Cord's hot-tempered lips and hissed, "So did you." She turned her blond head. "The program is about to begin."

He glanced about, catching the dulling glances of now-uninterested spectators. Settling back in his seat, he stewed alone in his own juices of self-conceit. He hated moments like this.

His stomach muscles clenched, and it took all of his acting ability to maintain his outward aura of calm. When would Deanna finally tell the story that would topple his world?

In the control booth high above the sparkling spectacle, the director spoke into his headset, instructing the stage manager below.

The stage manager held up a hand and gave the five-second countdown to airtime. The house lights dimmed, and the last-minute stragglers picked up their pace and hurried back to their seats.

The director commanded, "Close up on the emcee, camera two. Ready two. Take two."

The red camera light came on and Richard Crystal— renowned for both his meteoric rise in comedy as well as his humanitarian work with the homeless—smiled into the camera.

"Welcome back., ladies and gentleman. I hope you've enjoyed the first half of our awards ceremony. But if you haven't, just think, you only have one more half to go!"

The crowd erupted in laughter and began clapping.

"If you weren't aware, this is the first Grammy Awards ceremony that is broadcast around the world. There's a reason. Tonight is not just an event to recognize music, the artists, and the industry, but to pay tribute to a woman who has touched the world with her musical genius and her generosity of spirit, despite her own adversities."

Behind him a huge movie screen was filled with the smiling sand-toned face of Deanna Winters, her mint-green eyes looking boldly out into the audience. A thunderous roar of applause reverberated throughout the famous hall.

"What's happening?" Deanna whispered to Tracy.

"They've just put up a larger-than-life-size picture of your ugly mug—from the cover of your last album—on a movie screen, and the crowd is loving it for some strange reason."

Deanna nudged Tracy in the side with her elbow. "Very funny." She tucked in the smile that tickled her lips.

As she listened to the accolades being bestowed upon her, she could hardly relate them to herself. She did what she did because she wanted to, needed to, in a way not for the recognition. It was part of the reason why she'd stayed out of the public eye, away from media hounds, and had ceased performing in public. She swallowed back the lump of her reality—the real reason that she'd never shared—not even with Clay, at least in the beginning. She straightened her shoulders and wondered if he'd made it. He'd promised he would. Tonight, decisions would be made. Decisions that had the potential to change the rest of their lives—and she still wasn't sure what her decision would be. Maybe the next few hours would be the test.

"The Academy is proud to have with us tonight a great lady, a legend in her own right, who wants to pay tribute to a woman who has touched her," the emcee continued, bringing Deanna back from the turn of her thoughts. "We've heard her moving words enthrall the world at the inauguration of President Clinton. Her books and poetry have mesmerized generations. Ladies and gentlemen, Pulitzer Prize winner and poet laureate Dr. Maya Angelou."

Deanna's hand flew to her mouth to stifle the gasp that rushed to escape. The very idea that a woman whom she'd admired for most of her life was there to honor her brought Deanna to the brink of tears.

She wished she could see Dr. Angelou in all her regal glory step up to the podium. But she could imagine as the doctor's familiar, rich voice filled the theater.

Listening to Dr. Angelou extol her virtues and the wonderful work that she'd done around the world for people with disabilities, how she'd used her music to heal, her money to wage war on bureaucracy, and her own personal battles, caused the tears to finally flow.

Tracy turned and saw the silent tears trickle down the high arch of Deanna's cheeks. Tears that made Tracy smile. Deanna was the only person she'd ever known who never shed a tear of sadness, self-pity, or regret. Her tears were rivers of joy, and she had every reason to be happy tonight. She deserved it more than anyone.

"I...just can't believe it. Tracy. That's Maya Angelou up there, talking about me." Deanna grinned like a little kid with candy.

Tracy squeezed Deanna's hand. "You haven't heard nothin' yet, my sistah. Just you wait."

Dr. Angelou finished her speech with a moving poetic dedication to Deanna. The proceeds from the sale of the poem would be added to the Deanna Winters Foundation, she said.

The crowd rose, only to be further blown away by the musical tribute to Deanna featuring Quincy Jones, Herbie Hancock, Stevie Wonder, Patti Labelle. Gladys Knight, Ray Charles, and Kenny G. Together, the performers enthralled the audience with renditions of Deanna's own compositions, the music that had earned her three Grammy Awards and had changed the course of classical jazz. As the historic gathering of musical genius played, the screen ran a montage of Deanna's life, from her early days at Juilliard, her concert performances at the Metropolitan Opera, her Grammy wins, to her triumphant win of the Gold Cup in a riding competition in Surrey, England.

Cord Herrera listened, letting the power of the music and the images of the past carry him away. He let his mind float, his spirit ease. Her music was the one thing that always connected them—him and Deanna. Her music soothed his soul, put out the fires, cast out the demons.

But the magic never lasted.

Hearing the acclaim and what sounded like super-human feats attributed to Deanna made him smile, partly in pleasure, partly in regret. He too knew Deanna, in the most intimate of ways. He knew the Deanna that was shielded from the world. The Deanna that had shared a part of his life, his bed, and his dark secrets—before she was the Deanna she'd become. Before the accident.

CHAPTER II

In the Beginning

Even as the spotlight shone down on the stage, capturing the montage of musical legends, Cord could no longer stay focused on the unfolding events. Instead, all he could think about was sitting in this exact auditorium a little more than five years ago when the world stood up and took notice of him…at least for a time.

"Mr. Herrera." The headset-wearing attendant hesitated to touch. Instead he spoke again. Louder. "Mr. Herrera."

Cord snapped his head toward the offending hissing of his name.

"You're needed backstage. You're the alternate presenter for Artist of the Year. The one 'Formerly Known As' couldn't make it."

The now harried attendant pressed a hand to the earpiece of his headset, listened to instructions, then gestured for Cord to follow him.

Cord bounced between annoyance—that he should he an alternate—and unbridled delight that soon more than half the planet would see him live.

Ha! The understudy runs away with the lead. This was too good to be true, but couldn't have happened at a more opportune juncture in his career. He was on.

Cord eased out of his seat, said his "excuse mes," humping knees along the way as he followed the attendant out of the theater and backstage.

Cord could see relief glisten in the stage manager's eyes when he strolled in, relaxed and fully in control.

"Oh, thank God you were in your seat. When Richard calls your name, you go right through this curtain." The stage manager pointed to his left. "Walk to the podium and look directly into the TelePrompTer and read it exactly. Then you'll he joined onstage by the members of En Vogue. The four of you will name the contenders. After you name each contender, a short video will flash behind you. Then you open the winning envelope. When the winner comes onstage, congratulate him—or her, whatever, hand over the trophy, and step to your left. You will leave with the winner after the acceptance speech." He grinned broadly. "You have all that, Mr. Herrera?"

Cord gave him a long look of disgust. "I'm a professional, Mr. Whoever-you-are."

The stage manager's long nose went up into the air. "Fine. Listen for your cue."

The emcee was creating a comic uproar that seemed to last for hours as Cord stood poised, listening for his big moment. Trying to quiet the audience, the emcee switched gears. "And if that's not enough, tonight a bright new talent on the horizon, *People* magazine's 'Sexiest Man Alive,' the women's choice, is here to present the Artist of the Year Award. Cord Herrera!"

Cord strode across stage to the podium and shook the emcee's hand.

The roar of applause pumped through his bloodstream, fueling him with the adoration he craved. Deserved. He was finally alone with his audience.

For several breathtaking moments he stood in front of the hundreds in the theater, smiling his famous smile, nodding and waving to his fans until they finally quieted.

The now silent audience sat poised on the precipice of revelation. He, Cord Herrera, held the attention of the world in his hands. The awesomeness of this single moment momentarily stunned him. Then he saw the telltale red light go on above the TelePrompTer.

"This year," he began in the slight accent reminiscent of the actor Antonio Banderas, whom many said he resembled, "the music industry allowed us to soar to new and greater heights of expression than ever believed possible. We peered into our souls and found the light within. Once illuminated, it was not the cold, dank, desolate waste known for its inhumanity. These artists have embodied ideals within their music and have produced a real change that far exceeds the monetary bounty of their popularity. The nominees for the Artist of the Year are…"

The members of En Vogue stepped up to the microphone and read off the names: "Babyface for *Always*. Quincy Jones for *Get to This*. Deanna Winters for *Turning Point*. Donna Haze for *Lightning*. And Oleta Adams for *In My Lifetime*."

Cord stepped back to the mic and opened the envelope. He took a long moment, making the world hold its breath, like in the climax of one of his movies. "And the winner for Artist of the Year is…Deanna Winters for *Turning Point*."

The audience erupted in a roar of applause. Flashbulbs pierced the room with electric bolts of blinding light. The people were on their feet. The noise was deafening.

Who was so important, so magnetic as to draw the power of this response?

The magical strains from her album played in the background while the huge television screens projected larger-than-life images of Deanna Winters in concert, Deanna winning the Gold Cup for her equestrian feats, Deanna at the White House.

"Ladies and gentleman, Deanna Winters." The off-stage announcer's godlike voice hushed the crowd as a lone spotlight shone upon and followed the approaching figure who appeared to float up the stairs to the mammoth stage.

For that brief instant, Cord focused his full attention on someone other than himself. As she approached and looked up into his eyes, her green ones like twinkling emeralds, her scent a whisper from heaven, her body one that he would make love to endlessly, he lost a part of himself.

She tiptoed and embraced him, her supple body momentarily locking with his, and he felt a sudden and powerful erection that startled him with its force. Stunned, he barely heard her whispered words of thanks to him. She turned and faced her audience.

Cord was totally bewitched.

The after-party was a medley of celebrities, all of whom Cord knew on a first-name basis. He mingled, posed for the required photos as he worked the room, kissed all the right cheeks, talked to all the right people, all the while keeping a subtle eye on Deanna. She was out of her element, though she played the game well, he noted, following her movements over the rim of his champagne flute. She seemed anxious, almost edgy, though always polite, giving that smile of hers to all who approached her with words of congratulations. He liked that. She had class. Something that was lacking in most women he bedded.

Casually, he worked his way across the room until he was behind her.

"Enjoying yourself?"

She turned, the ever-ready smile on her face. "Oh, yes. It's wonderful."

Cord stepped closer, close enough to catch again the scent of her perfume. He dipped his head closer to her ear. "Tell the truth. This is awful and your jaws ache from smiling." He grinned mischievously. "I know mine are."

"These things are exhausting," she confessed, her smile almost as mischievous as his. "But it would be rude of me not to show up. Everyone is really very nice."

"I know what you mean. I've been to so many, but they never get any easier." He took a sip of champagne. "Can I get you a refill? You've been nursing that glass all evening."

She blushed. "You've been watching me."

"Can you blame me? You're a beautiful woman." His eyes rolled over her form encased in a body-hugging Versace gown that matched the unique green of her eyes. "A woman I want to know better."

"Are you always so direct with women you don't know?"

"As an actor, I adapt to the situation." He stepped closer, cutting her off from the rest of the room. "Just imagine how things could be when I do get to know you. But, of course, it is your choice. I'm sure you have someone…special who occupies your time. He should be here with you tonight. Celebrating your triumph."

Her breathing quickened just a notch, Cord noticed. He was having an effect on her, even though she tried to pretend otherwise.

"How do you know I'm *not* here with someone?"

Cord smiled. "Remember, I've been watching you all evening." She fought back a smile and lowered her gaze.

"Would you like to go out on the rooftop? See the stars? A star such as you should be among them." He sipped his champagne.

This time she laughed outright. "I bet you say that to all the girls." She turned and led the way out.

Cord followed closely behind. This was going to be a wonderful evening after all, he thought.

"I must admit, Deanna, I have never listened to any of your music." He leaned against the rooftop railing and looked at her. "But I will have to make it a point to do so if tonight is any indication of your talent."

"I guess you can say we're even," she parried, smiling slightly.

"I've never seen any of your pictures, and *you* have an Oscar."

"Touché." He saluted her with his glass. "I suppose we've both been too involved in our own worlds."

She nodded, then looked off to the horizon. "I don't have much time for anything. Between rehearsals, riding, training…there's just not enough time."

"But you must find time for yourself. *chica*. To travel, relax. What is fame and fortune if you're too busy to enjoy it?"

She looked at him for a long moment but said nothing, then turned her gaze back to the night sky. "I suppose you're right," she said on a soft breath. She took a sip of her champagne. "When you do something for so long, live your life a certain way, you don't even think that there could be more. You sort of accept things…the way they are."

She angled her head to face him as she leaned against the railing…Her eyes were wide and searching, or so it seemed to him.

"You live a difficult life, Deanna Winters. I lived that way once. So I know. I wasn't happy, and neither are you." His gaze lingered on her face. "Tell me I'm wrong."

He watched her try to form the words to deny what he'd said, but she couldn't. His mouth lifted on one side.

"Why don't we change that? You and me. I'll be in the states for another week or so before I go on location to film my next movie. I want to see you again. But only if you want to see me," he added with a quick grin, one that drew the response he had hoped for.

He ran his finger down her cheek. "Now that's more like it. A beautiful smile on a beautiful woman."

"You're quite the flatterer."

Cord dramatically clasped his chest. "You wound me. I only tell the truth."

Deanna tossed her head back and laughed. "Bravo. That was quite a performance."

Cord took a deep bow. He extended his hand. "Dance with me." She slipped her hand into his and stepped into his embrace.

They danced under the stars to Luther's "Going Out of My Head" drifting softly up from the party room. Cord inhaled the soft scent of her that sent his hormones reeling, felt every luscious curve of her slender body, the silk of her ink-black hair as it brushed his cheek. On the surface she gave the impression of being fragile. But her body was taut, refined, conditioned. She was anything but fragile. She couldn't be. Not in the business she was in. The music industry would eat you alive if you were weak. And to ride the way he'd heard she could took physical skill. The combination of sultry femininity, hard body, and talent fueled his libido.

He dared to pull her a bit closer. "You dance wonderfully."

"So do you," she whispered, looking up at him.

"We must make it a point to do this again." He brushed a tendril of hair away from her face. "Do you dance often?"

She shook her head.

"Then we'll change that. Won't we." It wasn't a question. "What makes you think I want things to change?"

"Everyone wants change, Deanna Winters," he crooned. "We must just be prepared for it when it happens. *Sí*?"

He sent a box of long-stemmed white roses to her home in Connecticut every day for a week before he finally called. Flowers were always a way to a woman's heart, he thought as he picked up the phone and dialed her number. She answered on the first ring, almost as if she was anticipating his call. As he'd hoped.

"I hope you haven't forgotten me," he said in greeting.

Deanna's musical laughter filled the phone lines. "How could I?"

"I'm reminded of you every time I look around my house that has turned into a flower shop." Her voice softened. "Thank you, Cord. They're beautiful."

"It's nothing. Just something to make you smile."

"Then you've succeeded."

"What are you doing? Right now. Right this minute."

"Going over a song I was writing. Why?"

"Get dressed for a night out. Don't ask questions. I'll be there in an hour."

"But—"

"No buts, as you Americans say. Time for some fun. As I promised."

"Cord—"

"See you in an hour. Wear something fabulous." He hung up, leaned back against the overstuffed pillows of his hotel bed and smiled.

The game had begun.

An hour later, a chauffeur arrived at Deanna's door and escorted her to the waiting limousine. When she stepped inside the cool, semi-darkened interior Cord greeted her with a flute of champagne.

She smiled, her eyes sparkling with delight. "Cord, you are too much. What is going on?"

He tilted her chin toward him and kissed her softly on the lips.

"Nothing is too much for you. And no questions. Just sit back and enjoy." He tapped the glass partition, and the driver pulled out of her long driveway onto the street.

"You look wonderful." He ran a hand along her shoulder. "Hmm. Silk does wonderful things for the body." He felt her tremble beneath his fingertips, and smiled. "Drink your champagne. There's plenty and I have a long, wonderful night planned."

"I have a rehearsal in the morning."

"And rehearsal will be there when you arrive. They cannot rehearse without their star. Correct?"

She took a tiny sip of champagne.

"So relax. Forget about work, schedules, and other people. Let's spend the evening on us. Does that suit you?"

"How can I say no?"

"Exactly." He kissed her again. A bit longer this time, then pulled away. "Do you enjoy starlit nights and sandy beaches?"

"Yes. But I don't get the chance to enjoy them very often."

"Then you will tonight."

They talked casually during the half-hour ride, with Cord regaling her with anecdotes of his movie escapades.

"You live a wild life, Cord. Don't you ever get tired of having to be 'on' all the time, being chased by photographers and reporters making up stories about you?"

He shrugged. "Unfortunately it's the nature of the business I'm in." He emitted a short laugh. "In my home in Argentina, I was just like everyone else. Poor, hungry, starving for attention in an overcrowded household. I had to fight to be noticed. My mother died after she had me, and my father spent the rest of his life blaming me for that."

"I'm sorry."

"My six sisters took care of me. So, of course, my father said I was spoiled. Weak." He tossed back the last of his drink and quickly refilled his glass. "This life of mine that you think is so, how do you say…hectic…it fills a need, sweet Deanna. You understand?"

She looked at him, really looked at him. "In that I guess we're alike. My whole life was spent in one rehearsal studio after the other. My parents believed that giving me things was the answer to not being around to love me. So I lived in a world of prep schools and every kind of 'lesson' imaginable." She sighed. "I'd been to more countries by the time I was twelve than most people would in two lifetimes. You at least had your sisters. Most of the girls I met in school either resented me because of my talent, or because I looked white."

The last remark didn't surprise him. He knew all too well about prejudice. He'd experienced it himself when he first arrived in America.

"I never had anyone until I met my friend Tracy," she added.

"But by that time, I was in graduate school. She was like my first real family."

"You say we are alike. But you've had all the things I've always wanted. You've had them since you were a child."

"Yes, material things. But neither of us was happy with what we had. We had to find our own way. Your acting fulfills you, makes you happy. That's how I feel about my music and my riding. It fills a need."

He angled his body so that he faced her. "Have you never had anyone, someone special, to fill that need, Deanna? Tell me," he softly urged. "The truth."

She swallowed, pressing her lips together. "No."

"We will change that, too." He stroked the side of her face with a fingertip. "You'll see."

The car slowed to a halt, and the chauffeur came around to open the door.

Deanna peered outside, then jerked her head back in the car.

"We're at an airport!"

Cord grinned mischievously. "Yes, it appears so. Come, let's see what else is in store for us tonight."

Within moments, he'd whisked her onto his private plane and they were up in the air, the lights of the city disappearing beneath them like so many candles blown out after a birthday wish.

"Cord. Where in the world are we going?"

"Now if I told you, it would take away the fun of the surprise," he teased.

A hostess came around and offered a plate of hors d'oeuvres and another round of champagne.

Cord placed a light kiss at Deanna's temple. "Just relax. The evening is young."

When they deplaned about an hour and a half later, they were again whisked away in a limo and got out in front of a breathtaking beach house.

Deanna took off her shoes to wiggle her toes in the white sand.

"Now will you tell me where we are?"

"We're on the far side of St. Kitt in the Virgin Islands." He extended a hand toward the house. "This is my private hideaway. The place where I come to evade the reporters, the photographers, the stress of life. Come, let me show you around."

Taking her by the hand, he gave her the grand tour of the two-story glass and stucco structure with its private pool in the back, expansive living room, den, four bedrooms, and three full baths.

"This is the kitchen," he said at the end of the tour. "I hardly use it, but it's fully stocked." He turned to her. His voice dropped an octave. "I gave the servants the night off." He saw her face flush. "So we will have a chance to get to know each other without interruption."

"Cord...I..."

He held up his hand. "Please do not worry. This is all above-board." He grinned. "And I'll have you back in plenty of time for your rehearsal. The stories you may have heard about me are far from true."

"To tell the truth, I don't read the gossip columns."

"That's even better. Then I don't have to try so hard to change your opinion. We can start fresh."

She smiled.

"Let me put on some music. Is there anything special you want to hear?"

"I'd rather see what your taste in music is like."

Cord put on an array of musical selections, from Soca, R&B, to Deanna's favorite, classic jazz. They danced, they talked, they laughed. Cord found himself revealing things to her that he had with no one else, and he didn't quite understand why. She just seemed so easy to talk with, eager to listen, really listen, not like the other women he'd been with, the ones who were eager to be in his company. Maybe she was different. But how could that be? All women were the same. She was just better at hiding it than the others.

So he was only mildly surprised when he led her to his bedroom and she didn't resist.

The pulsing strains from her own CD followed them up the winding staircase, floating over the clothing that fell piece by piece on the steps. In his bedroom, illuminated only by the full moon, her partially nude body looked as if it had been sculpted by an artist's hand. The roar of adrenaline rushed through his limbs, and he wanted to take her, then, there, on the floor. But he fought down the urge, knowing that he'd have to be slow…at least the first time.

He stepped close, felt the raw heat flow from her body. The soft scent of her filled his nostrils. Inhaling deeply, he reached out to stroke her bare shoulders. When she closed her eyes and shivered, he wrapped his arms around her, taking her mouth in one swift motion. Her soft moan inflamed and aroused him.

He rocked his hips against her, deep in the juncture of her slightly parted thighs. She clung tighter, almost as if she were afraid of falling. He slid one strap from her shoulder and then the other, pushing her lacy black bra downward, forcing her breasts up to his waiting mouth. Dipping his head, he took one hard tip and nicked his tongue teasingly across it, then the other, back and forth, pulling the heart of her heat tightly against his slowly gyrating hips until she cried out his name in a gush of agony and ecstasy.

Moving one hand from her firm derriere, he slid his fingers into the tangle of lightly woven hair, easily finding her wet center to taunt and tease the tiny bud until her body shook and trembled with the need to be filled.

"Oooh, Deanna," he groaned in her ear. "So sweet. I want you now, my way," he said in a ragged whisper, pushing her black panties down her trembling thighs. He backed her toward the bed, his mouth feasting on a ripe breast.

He trailed his tongue down her chest to her stomach, dipping into her navel. He inhaled her womanly scent. He eased down further until he buried his head between her legs. He held her hips in a viselike grip when she tried to pull away. The more she resisted, the more he pursued, until she was weak and wanting, digging her fingers into his shoulders, pushing him deeper into her realm. He pulled away and stood, kissing her long and hard, letting her taste her own essence. Then he lowered her to the bed, spreading her thighs with a sweep of his leg.

He looked into her eyes and smiled at the sparkling emeralds that gazed back at him. "Touch me." He took her hand and wrapped it around his pulsating shaft.

"Y-e-s-s." he hissed between his teeth. "For you. All for you."

Bracing his weight on his arms, her long legs draped over his shoulders, he lowered his body until he met the moist entryway. He pushed ever so gently, feeling her walls open. Deeper he pushed, until he met resistance. He pushed harder, and she moaned and clung tighter. He pulled his head back and looked at her. *No. Impossible.*

"Deanna?"

"I've...never..."

"Sssh. It will be all right. I promise." He covered her mouth with his, using his tongue to still the cry he knew would come, and pushed, hard, breaking through the thin barrier that separated them.

Her body tightened and bucked against his. She tried to cry out, but he deepened his kiss and held her firmly as her body adjusted to his. Then he began to move inside her, slow and easy until her trembling stopped and she began to pick up his rhythm. She moaned softly as he placed tiny kisses across her face, stroked her body as they rode together.

"Yes, my sweet Deanna," he groaned, the onset of his climax beginning to build. He lifted her then and stood, still buried deep within her, and carried her to the far side of the room, pressing her against the wall. And he forgot about being gentle, going slow, his own need for satisfaction rushing to his brain like a potent drug. He suckled the tender skin of her neck, took tiny nips on her swollen breasts, and thrust harder, faster, deeper, feeling the power. Her cries of his name only propelled him, like the applause he craved, the adoration he sought, until the last drop of his immortality was spent, and they collapsed in a tangle of damp limbs on the carpeted floor.

That's all any of them wanted, he thought as the satiation of sex lulled him to sleep. They were all the same.

But as the days passed, weeks turned into months, Cord began to realize that she *was* different. She was special. A genuine caring person. But could he be? The thought frightened him. Yet fear couldn't keep him away from her.

Whenever he was in town, he spent all of his free time with her. Whenever she could, she traveled to where he was filming. Their faces appeared in every newspaper and magazine as the hottest couple of the decade. At times her fame seemed to eclipse his, and those were the times when the long years of loneliness and frustration, years of struggling for love and adoration. exploded in raw, physical release.

Deanna had just finished a tour that ended at the Kennedy Center in Washington, D.C. The sounds of "bravo" and "more" still rang in the air when he met her backstage.

He slid an arm around her waist, leaned down and kissed her mouth in unison with the pop of flashbulbs from photographers' cameras, greedily surrounding the famous duo.

"Ms. Winters, where to next? Now that your tour is over, are you going to England? Will you be competing at Ascot?"

Deanna looked at the reporter and smiled. "Yes, I will. I've been looking forward to riding Dreammaker in the competition for months."

"Do you think you'll bring home another gold cup?" asked a reporter from *The Washington Post.*

"All I can do is give it my best. Some of the greatest riders in the world will be competing."

A microphone was thrust at Cord. "With your new film coming up, Mr. Herrera, will you be accompanying Ms. Winters?"

Cord turned and faced the reporter and the television cameras.

"My next film, *Absolution,* is scheduled to go into production in about six weeks." He turned slightly to his left, mindful of projecting his best side. "But I do intend to be with Deanna for the opening events."

"What about marriage? Are there wedding bells in your future?"

Cord flashed the smile that had melted the hearts of millions of women. He briefly looked at Deanna. "No comment." He grinned, holding up his hand to forestall any further questions. "Now, if you all don't mind, Deanna and I are very tired."

Shielding her from the onslaught with a protective arm around her bare shoulders, Cord hurried them down the long corridor, out into the balmy night and to the waiting limousine.

"Champagne," Cord stated more than asked, settling himself in the plush velvet comfort of the Lincoln's cozy interior. He poured Dom Perignon into two crystal flutes and handed Deanna the sparkling liquid.

He watched her. "You still wrinkle your nose at the taste of champagne. Even after all this time."

"I only drink it because it's expected. I'd rather have a glass of iced tea or lemonade."

Cord chuckled. "One of these days, sweet Dee, you'll accept the pleasures of the good life that you've aspired to. Drink up."

She only smiled and rested her head against the upholstery.

Her eyelids drooped wearily, and Cord let her be. Performances were exhausting.

The limo slowed to a stop in front of the notorious Watergate Hotel, the site of former President Nixon's fall from American grace. The driver opened the door, helping Deanna to her feet.

"We won't need you until tomorrow afternoon to take us to the airport, Paul," Cord said to his personal driver. "You should plan to be here by noon."

"Yes, sir." He tipped his hat. "Good night, Ms. Winters, Mr. Herrera."

"Goodnight, Paul. Have a pleasant evening." Deanna smiled at the stately driver.

Cord brushed by him without a word or a backward glance, pushing through the revolving glass doors of the hotel. "I still have no idea why you spend time on pleasantries with the hired help." He shook his head, perplexed.

"And I still don't see why you can't. They're people, too. Decency will take you a long way in life, Cord."

"Humph. So you keep saying."

Once inside the confines of the opulent hotel room, Cord quickly discarded tie and jacket onto the arm of the couch, shoes in the middle of the white carpeted floor, and began unbuttoning his tuxedo shirt, which landed next to his jacket, then slipped to the floor. He was so accustomed to having someone, maids, personal assistants, six sisters, pick up after him that he expected it wherever he went. Disarray didn't faze him. It seemed to drive Deanna to distraction, however. And as hard as he tried to get her to see the wonders that wealth and stature could bring her, the more she seemed to resist. She had never known what it was like to be without, to have to scrape for every nickel, a piece of bread.

But he had known poverty. Now he would never want for anything in life again. He deserved everything he'd achieved. And one day his father would finally say he was proud of his only son.

He watched Deanna in all her quiet, proud splendor walk out of the room, and suddenly he became angry. Angry that she seemed content with her life, her world, her accomplishments. She never seemed to want more. People loved her wherever she went. She didn't have to try to charm, to please. It was as natural as the stunning green of her eyes, the flawlessness of her skin. But he wanted her to bend to him, to need him, to adore him like all the other women. He wanted her to submit to him. And no matter what he did, there always remained a thin veil between them. The only time he felt that she was totally his to do with as he wished was when he made love to her. When he took her against her will. Then he was in control. *He* was the star. And she cried and pleaded, just like all the others. Then she was his.

Crossing the room, he stood in the doorway of the bedroom and watched her remove her clothing. She unzipped her gown, letting it slide into a shimmering pool at her feet. She stepped out of it, bent to retrieve it, then hung it on a padded hanger next to her array of designer gowns and tailored suits. Funny, he thought, she always seemed more comfortable in faded jeans and a sweatshirt.

She stepped over to the stereo and put on her latest CD, swaying gently to the music. Clad in her black, strapless demi-bra and matching panties, she plucked at the hairpins that held her thick, ink-black hair in a French roll. A toss of her head and the natural waves tumbled around her shoulders.

"Now that's how I like to see you."

She turned, and her eyes rested on his bare, bronzed chest. She swallowed as he slowly approached. He walked up to her, coming so close he could feel her fear. She looked up at him with that mixture of apprehension and helplessness brimming in her eyes, that look that he loved to see. Her body trembled as his smile widened. Usually at times like this, when his anger, his frustration overwhelmed him, the thought of her music, the magic in her fingers, the sounds that rang in his head, soothed the savage fire raging in his soul. Not tonight. He didn't want to hear the music.

Roughly he pulled her to him, his muscled arms like a vise around her tiny waist. He rocked and thrust his pelvis fervently against her, making her moan, heightening his pleasure.

His mouth came down on her neck, biting the skin. With his free hand he cupped her breast, squeezing and kneading, rubbing the turgid nipple until it could peak no more.

"Cord…please…"

Her cry fell on deaf ears. He was too consumed by his own boiling lust, needing to sate his sexual greed as desperately as he needed to be fulfilled by the roar of the millions who paid homage to him on the big screen.

He ignored her cries when he shredded her hose and ripped the bikini panties. Nor did he hear her pleas when he entered her unprepared body and began his flight to relief.

He never did.

When Cord strode into the bedroom the following morning, Deanna was standing in front of the full-length mirror gently running her hands along her neck. Cord eased up behind her, pressing his body close to hers. He felt the tension ripple through her as her body stiffened. Seductively he placed tiny kisses along her neck.

"You should cover these up," he whispered, pressing his mouth against the purplish bruises on her neck and those that dotted her breasts. "Everyone doesn't need to know how passionate we are with each other."

She began to button her jacket. He stilled her fingers, running his hand across her right breast and lovingly caressing it.

He was getting hot again. He wanted her. He never seemed to get enough of her, no matter how many hours it took. Maybe it was because she always seemed remote, there in body but not in spirit. He lifted her hair from the back of her neck and kissed her there, pressing just a little closer. All he wanted was for her to love him. He turned her to face him.

Her gaze was indifferent, and it only fueled him. He began unbuttoning the remaining buttons of her V-neck, collarless jacket, revealing the bareness beneath. She didn't move.

"Just a few minutes," he groaned, then fastened his mouth to her breasts.

"The car will be here any minute, Cord," she said, as calmly as if reciting the weather.

He pulled away, reality setting in. He had no intention of missing his night. Sabrina, the leading lady in his next film, was waiting for him at his home in Los Angeles. Yes, Sabrina would gladly take the edge off, and maybe he could put Deanna to the back of his mind. At least for a while.

Sitting in the back of the limo, Cord rubbed her thigh. "You were wonderful last night, Dee. I wish that we would have had time this morning."

Deanna remained silent.

He rubbed a little harder, and her body stiffened beneath his fingertips. "If you'd just let go, you'd enjoy it more too." He leaned over and kissed her cheek. "You will in time. We'll just have to work at it."

She simply smiled.

They did not speak the rest of the way to Dulles International Airport. Another of many silent rides these past weeks. When they arrived, Cord held Deanna's hand possessively as they made their way through the mazelike airport terminal, breezing by would-be gawkers and autograph hounds. He and Deanna hid behind dark glasses, which did little to disguise them. Deanna, clad in her Donna Karan white linen pantsuit, matching mules, all-purpose straw bag, and animal print scarf, stood out like a runway model. Just the way he liked her to look. Many mistook her for the actress Salli Richardson from the movie *Posse.* Deanna's easy grace and natural beauty were perfect matches to Cord's dark, brooding good looks and challenging swagger.

They arrived at Deanna's gate first. Cord snaked an arm around her waist, turning her to face him. Slowly, he removed her dark glasses and stuck one end of the stem down the opening or her jacket, anchoring them between her breasts.

His midnight eyes met jade. "I'll see you in two weeks." Cord titled up Deanna's dimpled chin, and took a long, slow kiss. "Maybe sooner."

Her smile seemed forced. She pecked him on the lips. "You'll miss your plane."

He stepped back, his eyes rolling over her one last time. "Call me when you get in."

"I will." She turned toward the gate, moving along with the passengers. "I promise," she called over a man's head.

Cord watched her until she disappeared, then headed for his departure gate. *One day, Deanna,* he silently swore, you will be mine. *Totally.*

CHAPTER III

When Cord levered out of his Olympic-size pool, water dripped like champagne from his nude, bronzed frame. He looked up. For once, the skies of Los Angeles were clear. The stars actually twinkled. Cord smiled as he strode toward the glass doors leading to the house. He hadn't spoken to Deanna in several days and had been unable to reach her by phone. But it was just as well. He had plenty to occupy his time. Between rehearsals for the movie and his late-night activities, he had successfully been able to banish her from his thoughts, which was what he wanted.

He pushed open the glass doors and stepped inside, dripping water along the way. Even after a year in their relationship, he still had been unable to capture Deanna's heart. Yet, she stayed with him. She listened to him tell of his fears, his rantings about his success. She soothed him with her music when he fell into bouts of depression, or erupted into rages, letting him empty his loneliness into her body. She'd even suggested that he get counseling to help him deal with his feelings of alienation from his father. But he couldn't do that. That would prove his father right—that he was weak. So he sought other means to fill the constant void in his soul. Like he would tonight. He had found an equal substitute to punish his father for not loving him.

He stepped into the partially darkened bedroom. Immediately spotting the outline of his latest conquest beneath the designer sheets. His heart thumped with exhilaration and fear. Exhilaration at the depravity of it and fear of discovery. He strode up to the bed, pulled back the sheet, and crawled in next to the warm, waiting body.

Immediately he could feel the charge running through his body like an electric current. He roughly turned his partner over and mindlessly thrust into that body from behind, pushing into it all the hurt and pain that he could never rid himself of…except at times like this. Like this.

And that was how Deanna found them.

From the bed, Cord gazed terrified into eyes that held no censure, only disappointment. Quietly she left the way she'd come, taking the remnants of her pride and his secret with her.

CHAPTER IV

Clay McDaniels watched the unprecedented outpouring of adoration on the small television in the back of the limousine, and his chest filled with unabashed pride. Never in his thirty-six years, his travels around the world and his acquaintance with everyone from shopkeepers to presidents and kings had he met anyone who could compare to Deanna. *His* Deanna.

They'd met nearly three years earlier when her Foundation was just getting off the ground and she was in the process of opening the Institute, a school for visually impaired children. He had expected that she'd be no different, no better than all the other self-absorbed, egotistical, micro-managing holders of wealth that he'd encountered in his lucrative business.

But the Deanna he'd come to know and love had, in her own inimitable style and grace, changed his skewed perspective, his jaded beliefs, and his life.

He tapped on the glass partition. "Please hurry Paul. I want to be there when she accepts her award."

He returned his gaze back to the screen. Watching the world peek into the panorama that was her life, he, at the moment, felt truly blessed to have been a part of the woman she'd become. Thinking of those early days still made his pulse quicken.

It all began when he had returned from Paris after transporting a cache of designer gowns and diamonds, which were to be unveiled at a spring fashion extravaganza. The show was set to the pace in fashion for the coming year, and he'd been paid a sinful sum to ensure that absolutely no one, including the pilot, flight crew, and those customs hound dogs got the slightest peek at the creations. He shook his head in amazement just thinking about the things people would pay money for.

Slinging his overnight bag over his shoulder, he stepped off the elevator and headed toward the heavy oak door that led to his suite of offices, having opted to go straight there instead of home. He rotated his stiff neck as he walked down the carpeted corridor. There was nothing to go home to anyway. Rachel had made sure of that. Involuntarily his stomach muscles knotted at the thought of his ex-wife. "Not today," he mumbled. "Don't go there."

He opened the door and was not surprised to see the two techies who manned the computers. Even though it was Saturday evening, the office was still humming with activity. In his business there were no days off and someone, usually him, had to be on call twenty-four-seven. He waved and nodded on his way to his office but stopped when he spotted Grace Duval in hers.

Grace was his office manager and ran the business like a military operation. She never seemed to mind the long hours, the quirky clients with their bizarre requests, or seeing to every minute detail of his elite courier service. Hell, if he didn't know better he'd think Grace Duval was an android. She never seemed to tire, she always had the answers, and he'd swear she never went home.

He eased on in and planted a big, sloppy kiss on her cheek. "How's tricks, Gracie?" He rested his hip on the edge of her black lacquer desk, one she'd insisted upon having and kept polished to an almost blinding gleam.

Grace peered up at Clay over her half-framed glasses, then slid them off the perch of her slender nose. She teased the pen tip between her teeth.

"Got an interesting phone call today, Boss Man."

"Are you gonna be cryptic or just blurt it out?" He plucked a lethally sharpened pencil from a small refurbished flowerpot that served as Grace's catchall bucket and twirled it between his fingers.

Grace pushed out a long breath and rolled her dark brown eyes as hard as she could. "I shouldn't tell you. I should just let Jason handle it."

He hopped down from his perch, then braced his hands on her desk and leaned intimately closer. "But whoever it is asked for me specifically and wouldn't take someone else," he taunted, biting back a mischievous chuckle.

"You know how much I *personally*," she emphasized, "hate it when you're right."

Clay let go of his laugh and Grace couldn't fight hers. She snatched the pencil from his fingertips and jammed it back into the pot.

"So, what gives? Who needs my services now?"

She paused for effect. "Does the name Deanna Winters ring any bells?"

It took several seconds for the bomb she'd dropped to detonate, and when it did, Clay hopped off the desk. His usual terse retorts were suffused by something akin to awe.

"Let me get this straight," he began, finding his tongue lodged somewhere in his throat. "*The* Deanna Winters…the musical genius…Grammy winner…*and* my favorite artist of all time, has requested my services? I thought she'd dropped off the face of the earth."

Grace was grinning from ear to ear. "She called personally. Said you'd been highly recommended and she'd like to meet with you to discuss the possibility of working with you."

"Her exact words?"

"Exactly. And she wants you to call her. Tonight. Even though I told her I wasn't sure how late you'd be. She said it didn't matter." And then Grace went for the jugular, pulling out a slip of message paper and dangling it under his nose like an evil child passing a plate of piping hot food in front of a starving man. "Her home number," she singsonged.

He snatched the paper from her fingers.

"Be nice," she warned.

"I got your nice," he retaliated, balling his fist and pressing it against her nose. He looked at the number, then stuck the paper in the pocket of his jacket, taking that moment of mundane activity to regain his perspective.

He'd met people of note before. Deanna Winters certainly wouldn't be the first. Yes, he was a devout fan of hers. Her innovations in classical jazz had made her a legend, setting her light-years ahead of other artists. He had every piece she'd ever recorded and he'd always had a secret desire to meet her.

But experience had taught him the harsh lessons of life; the rich and famous were one of the most difficult, egocentric, borderline psychotic people he'd ever met, who would sell their mamas if they thought they could write it off. But, hey, they paid the bills, which afforded him the chance to live the lavish lifestyle to which he'd grown quite accustomed. And on that note, he couldn't imagine that Deanna Winters was any different from the others. No matter that she seemed to have devoted herself to charity and fundraising, and for some reason, which escaped him at the moment, had stopped performing a couple of years earlier.

"I'll give her a call, Gracie. Anything else?"

"That's it for now. Well, aren't you excited? I don't think anyone has actually seen or spoken to her in nearly three years. And then *bam*, she calls you!"

"I'm sure she's just like all the other nuts we deal with, maybe worse since she's been in hibernation." He squinted in concentration, trying to recall what he'd read about her some years back. "Wasn't she in some sort of accident or something?"

"Riding accident. Blinded her."

The news hit him like a punch in the stomach. Old details came rushing back.

Grace sadly shook her head. "At the height of her musical career. Damn shame. That was one beautiful lady. Could have been a model. Wonder what she looks like now?" Clay slowly digested what he'd been told, bits and pieces about news of the accident becoming clearer. He seemed to remember one major article about it with sketchy details on her recovery, and then nothing—a media blackout. Until she semi-resurfaced with the Deanna Winters Foundation about a year ago.

Hmm. Wonder what does she look like now?

It was Sunday. It was hot and it was early. Too early to be out of the house, least of all out of bed. The trip, compounded with lack of enough sleep, had done a real number on him.

Clay almost groaned as he slid behind the wheel of his Benz. Every muscle in his body rebelled against the macabre trick he was playing on it. And every tendon, sinew, and blood vessel vigorously sent their protests straight to his head, which pounded mercilessly.

He backed the car out of his driveway and checked his directions to Ms. Winter's house on Central Park West in Manhattan. He snorted back his disgust, not so much because of the drive at the unholy hour of eight A.M., but his own spinelessness at not being able to just say no.

It had been right on the tip of his tongue. He could taste it, but she had sounded so sincere, so apologetic for infringing on his time, but she really needed to meet with him Sunday morning because she was scheduled to leave the country on an early afternoon flight. She'd even gone so far as to promise him an old-fashioned breakfast, which she would prepare herself.

That part he seriously doubted, and he had almost asked her how she intended to pull that off if she was blind, but caution jumped out of nowhere and cut him off. However, he'd never been one to turn down a meal. And truth be told, he really wanted to meet her.

The drive, which shouldn't have taken more than a half hour, turned into an hour long stop and go, horn honking, rubbernecking, name-calling exercise in misery.

He swerved around a slow-moving mile-long Cadillac and clenched his teeth in an effort to bite back a string of curses. The worst culprits were probably on their way to church service. He would laugh if his head wasn't hurting.

Finally, he pulled onto her block on Ninety-sixth Street, dotted by enormous trees and hedges standing sentinel in front of stately brownstones.

This was definitely the high end of town, the houses rivaling his brownstone in Harlem.

He'd put a lot of work into refurbishing and restoring his building. It had taken years and all of his free weekends to get it back to its original splendor with its stained-glass windows, parquet floors, and marble sinks. When it was finally finished, a small fortune spent in repairs and furnishings, Rachael walked out and filed for divorce. "Irreconcilable differences," she'd whined to her lawyer. The differences being, as far as she was concerned, they lived *too* far uptown in the wrong neighborhood. And his messenger-service business, still struggling at the time, was far beneath her, since the owner was no more than an errand boy.

So now he had a four-story brownstone worth at least a quarter of a million dollars that was empty save for him and his furniture.

That old familiar burning sensation singed his stomach. That was another lifetime. He'd come a long way from a mailman on Wall Street to the owner of a small messenger service to what he was now: president and sole owner of the most elite courier service in the world. But what did it all mean, anyway? he thought, stepping out of the car. Money, travel, prestige, and success—to enjoy—alone.

He shrugged off the disparaging thoughts. Today was not the day to wallow in self-pity and recriminations. Today was about getting Deanna Winters to see that *his* business was *her* business.

He confirmed the address in front of him with the number on a slip of paper, trotted up the short flight of steps to the front door, and rang the bell.

As he heard the delicate chimes trill through the house, he was suddenly nervous, as if he'd walked into class and was told there would be a pop quiz. A trickle of perspiration ran down the column of his back, and his pulse beat just a bit too fast for his taste.

"This is ridiculous," he mumbled. "Not the first time you're meeting folks." He took a deep breath just as the door was pulled open, and the breath he'd taken caught in his chest.

"Mr. McDaniels?"

The musical quality of her voice played along his nerve endings, awakening each and every one of them with her statementlike question. She was taller than he'd envisioned with the body of a model—long and sleek—and just curvy enough to spark curiosity about what lay beneath her obviously expensive attire. Her ink-black hair, lightly brushing across her shoulders, shimmered in the morning light.

"Yes, uh, Clay McDaniels."

The most beautiful smile spread across her rich mouth. "You have the voice of a preacher, Mr. McDaniels." A tiny dimple, that matched the one in her chin, teased her right cheek, and for the life of him, he'd swear she could see him with those sparkling green eyes. The fact that she didn't wear dark glasses really threw him. *Didn't blind people wear dark glasses?*

Deanna extended her hand. "I'm so glad you could come on such short notice."

Her hand was as smooth as silk. Probably never did a hard day's work in her life, he thought, dredging up anything negative he could summon to ward off the surge of unsettling sensations that set off his hormones.

"Please…come in," she entreated, still holding his hand. "You have strong hands, Mr. McDaniels. I like that. Is it indicative of your personality? No. Don't answer that. I'd like to find out for myself."

She led him through the front room, the living room, and into an almost restaurant-size kitchen.

"I have breakfast all prepared. It's the least I could do since I got you out of the house so early on a Sunday morning. Have a seat. It's buffet, as you can see." She chuckled. "At least I hope it is."

Clay was totally thrown off center. She seemed competent and in control. She had a sense of humor about her condition and was incredibly sensual without even trying. He knew she couldn't see, yet she maneuvered around furnishings and across thresholds like she had twenty-twenty vision. But there was no way he'd believe that she had prepared and laid out the fare before him.

There was a glass pitcher of what looked like freshly squeezed orange juice, so cold that moisture clung in tiny dewdrops along its potbellied middle. On a sterling silver warming tray, in the center of the linen-covered table, beef sausages, Virginia ham, and eggs that looked as light as clouds, made his stomach want to holler. *There had to be some household help around somewhere.* He looked casually around but didn't hear or see anyone.

"You're still standing," she said, snapping him out of his perusal. "Have a seat and help yourself to as much as you want. There's plenty." She opened the oven and removed a Pyrex dish filled with blueberry pancakes. Turning with the agility of a dancer, she placed the dish on the table and sat down.

Clay finally did likewise and began to slowly fill up his plate, keeping a close eye on Deanna in the meantime. He could hardly believe she was blind. She was bound to slip up at some point.

"Would you like to say the blessing?" she asked, appearing to look him straight in the eye.

"I'm not much of a praying man, but you…please do."

She nodded and inclined her head. Her soft words of thanks for a new day and the food before them were so simple, yet he sensed it went much deeper.

"I guess you're wondering why I called you, Mr. McDaniels." She took a mouthful of eggs and slowly chewed.

"I would assume that you need a job done and you've been told I'm the one who can do it."

Her right eyebrow arched, then relaxed. "Along with all of your other notable qualities, you don't mince words either."

He set down his glass. "I find it a waste of time, Ms. Winters. I prefer to be direct and to the point."

"Then let's get to the point. I'd like to engage your services in the handling of financial transactions that come into the Foundation. I understand you're bonded in the United States, Europe, and Africa."

"You've done your homework. But don't you have someone who handles that?"

"Why don't we finish our meal and then discuss my proposition over coffee in the living room?"

"You may not know this, Mr. McDaniels," she began, reaching to remove her coffee cup from the tray that rested on a cherrywood table between them. "But I rarely go out. I've ceased making public appearances, and I don't give interviews. What I do is use the resources that have become available to me to help others. That was the reason for launching the Deanna Winters Foundation."

"The Foundation has been operational for more than a year, correct?" He'd done some cursory research after receiving her message, but he was so tired last night he wasn't sure how much of it stuck.

"Yes, it has. And to avoid your next question, I need you because donations come in from all over the world. There are many donors who do not trust conventional means of delivery. They want to be assured not only that the Foundation receives their often enormous contributions, but that I *personally* receive them. Which brings me back to where I began. I don't go out much in public, and I prefer to remain as far behind the scenes as possible."

"In other words, if you can assure your donors that their money is going directly to you, it would satisfy your problem?"

"Yes. And I'm told you're the one who can make that happen."

He stared at her for a moment, and was convinced that she could see him. It was unnerving. He even waved his hand in front of her with no reaction. But what if she was faking this whole blind thing for some twisted reason? Everybody had a gimmick. Maybe this was hers. He would have to see for himself.

While her attention was diverted retrieving a beige envelope she'd placed on the table, as quietly as he could, he braced the side of his foot against a leather ottoman and pushed it out of position. Now it would block her path when she got up. If she couldn't see she'd trip right over it.

He took a sip from his cup. It was a vicious little trick, but he had to know for sure.

She held out the envelope. "This contains the information about the Foundation, a list of current donors, what

the Foundation funds, and anything else I thought would
be helpful."

She smiled hopefully. He took the envelope.

"After you go over the contents and I return form South
America, I hope we will meet again to discuss the terms of
an agreement between us."

"I thought you said you don't go out much." *Gotcha.*

"I don't. I make three to four major trips per year for
the initial contact with potential donors." She paused.
"Then I return here."

Something inside of him shifted. The wall he'd been
trying to keep between them chipped. It was the tone of her
voice, the hint of strain when she talked about the trips and
the hollowness when she talked about returning home. For
that brief moment, the light that seemed to radiate around
her dimmed.

He cleared his throat. "I see."

Suddenly she rose. "I've kept you long enough and I
can't tell you how much I appreciate your listening. I hope
you'll consider working with me. The Foundation, it's...it's
very important to me."

He could only stare at her, stare at the ottoman, and
mutter, "I see," once more.

She must have thought he didn't believe her, because
her posture became just a bit more regal, the tilt of her chin
just a bit higher. "I'm sure you have something in your life
that you're passionate about, Mr. McDaniels. That's how I
feel about the Foundation. There are millions of children
around the world who are disabled, and their families don't
have the resources to get them the kind of care and reha-

bilitation they need. I want to change that for as many children as I can.

"Yes, of course," he said quickly, never taking his eyes off her. One step...what if she fell? He'd feel like a monster. But he had to know. "I understand completely, Ms. Winters."

She took a breath and flashed the dimpled smile that played havoc with his hormones. "I'm sorry, Mr. McDaniels. I'm just running on. I'll walk you out."

Deanna turned and her shin connected with the ottoman. A startled cry. Hands flailing helplessly, she struggled to keep her balance.

Clay shot forward, his reaction so quick, so instinctive, he must have known deep inside what would happen. He grabbed her around the waist an instant before she pitched forward.

They both spoke at once.

"I'm sorry," Clay mumbled, righting her on her feet and keeping his hands on her, just in case.

"I haven't done that in—Oh, God, I'm so—I don't know this house like the back of my hand. I would never—"

Her head snapped toward him, realization dawning in wide green eyes. "The ottoman is out of place. You moved it. Didn't you?"

He felt the pounding of her heart against his palm, and he could not say a word. He felt sick. Disgusted with himself and his twisted need to probe her for gimmicks, for flaws.

"You moved it purposely." Blinking rapidly, she snatched herself free of his hold.

Fumbling in front of her, she bent and returned the ottoman to its rightful position.

She straightened. "Please leave. Better yet...get out. Now, Mr. McDaniels."

And still he could not speak. He saw her throat working as if she was having difficulty swallowing. Though he wasn't a praying man he prayed that the ground would open up and end this debacle now.

And then she spoke in a tone of deep sadness. "All my training, the hard work it took to make my life reasonably comfortable, you tried single-handedly to dismantle with one evil act. I was no longer a woman who was blind, but a blind woman to you." She took a breath. "But...Mr. McDaniels, I won't allow anyone to make me feel helpless and clumsy, someone to feel sorry for."

The kaleidoscope of emotions that flitted across her face made him sick with shame. "Ms. Winters, I...I don't know what to say. I...wasn't thinking."

"No. You weren't. You were too busy playing let's-trip-the-blind-girl games. *I'm* not the one you should feel sorry for." She squared her shoulders, turned her back to him. "I asked you to leave. I'm sure you can find your way out without any help from me."

Clay hung his head, not knowing what to say to make it right. With great reluctance he moved toward the front door, his steps cement-heavy with regret. "I'm sorry," he whispered, opening and closing the door softly behind him.

Clay drove mindlessly through the congested streets of Manhattan. He drove around Central Park oblivious to the riot of floral color, the young couples pushing baby carriages, Roller-bladers who challenged motorists and pedestrians with death-defying acrobatics, dogs who gave a leg up at every vantage point. He didn't smell the pungent aromas of freshly cut grass mixed with the sharp smell of gyros, hot sausages, and shish kebabs cooked on the corners by street vendors.

He slammed his fist against the steering wheel setting off the horn and causing an instantaneous cacophony of answering horns and medley of extremely rude gestures. He did not care.

How could he have done something so absolutely cruel? Had his view of life become so jaded that he honestly believed someone would pretend to be blind? Damn, he *should* kick himself. He should kick himself. He knew he'd hurt her. Not to mention the humiliation he'd obviously put her through. It had taken a lot for her to say what she had said, to confess what she'd endured, that she wouldn't allow him to destroy the confidence she'd so painfully gained. That took a special kind of person. A woman of substance. One he'd never met until today.

Clay's beeper went off the moment he set foot in his house. He pulled the tiny black box from the waistband of his pants and saw his office number flash across the L.E.D. screen.

"Now what?" he asked, not at all surprised to find his workaholic office manager on the job on a Sunday.

After being thoroughly chastised by Grace, he hung up the phone and still wasn't sure if he could believe what he'd just heard.

Deanna Winters had called his office. She still wanted to work with him, even though he was a first-class idiot. Now he really felt lower than dirt. That simple act gave him a sneak peek into the personality of Deanna Winters. The woman had class and integrity to spare. Maybe she could loan him some.

Even after what he'd pulled, she put her own pride and anger aside to ensure that the job got done. She knew what was important, which was more than he could say for himself.

He sat down heavily on the edge of his bed, then flopped back, tucking his hands beneath his head. He stared up at the stuccoed ceiling and a picture of Deanna when she opened the door for him danced before his eyes.

"You won't regret this, Ms. Winters," he vowed. "I promise you that."

CHAPTER V

"Good evening, Mr. McDaniels."

Clay stood on the steps of Deanna's townhouse feeling like a puppy with its tail between its legs. He'd rehearsed at least a dozen times what he would say when he saw her again. Standing here now, staring at this beautiful self-possessed woman, he could barely remember his manners.

"Good evening, I hope."

And then she smiled and he felt his insides shift.

"So do I. Please, come in."

"Can I get you anything before we get started?" she asked, leading him into the living room.

"No. Thanks." He took a seat on the couch and put his briefcase near his feet...out of her way.

"Is that Air, the Michael Jordan cologne, you're wearing?"

The question totally threw him, and for the moment his brain seemed to scramble. "Yes. It is."

She grinned. "And you're trying to figure out how I know." She sat down opposite him on the matching love seat and crossed her long legs at the knees. "When you lose one of your senses you learn to compensate with others. I've had to develop my sense of taste, smell and touch to a fine art. I happen to like Air and recognized it. You have good taste."

"Thank you." Was she flirting with him? Actually, he wished that she was.

"Now that you know a bit more about how I manage, let's talk about business."

"I'd like to get some things out of the way before we get started. I want to apologize for being such an ass. What I did was stupid and callous. I deeply apologize, Ms. Winters. I'm good at what I do when I'm not being an idiot. The best actually, and I'm glad you're going to give me the opportunity to prove it."

"Apology accepted." She paused. "I've learned over the years, Mr. McDaniels, that people distrust others because they've been betrayed or hurt in the past by someone close to them. They build up defenses and believe that everyone is trying to get one over on them, and their job is to do it first. That being my belief, I couldn't hold what you did against you."

He felt as if she'd looked deep into his soul and even though what she saw was dark and ugly, it was still all right. "You're a very remarkable woman."

"That I am," she said with a confident smile.

Clay chuckled. "Now that we have that out of the way, why don't you tell me what you need and how I can make it happen."

They talked for hours, with Deanna filling him in on the goal of the Foundation, which was to fund charitable organizations that dealt with pediatric blindness. One of her major projects was to set up the Institute, a training center that focused on visual rehabilitation using music therapy, with funds that came through the Foundation.

"I believe that if children learn to use music to express themselves, it's a step closer to building the confidence they need to function. Playing an instrument isn't something that you need your eyes to do. It's an avenue that the visually impaired can master and excel in. And I want to make sure that every child who needs a chance gets it."

"Do you plan to teach any of the classes?"

"No. I don't." She folded and unfolded her hands, then lowered her head before looking up.

Clay studied the nervous gestures, totally incongruous with the Deanna Winters he was coming to know. He thought it curious that she'd decided not to teach, especially considering her phenomenal talent.

He leaned forward, bracing his arms on his thighs. "This may be personal and totally out of line. If you decide not to answer I'll understand." He waited a beat. "Why did you stop playing, especially since you said that sight is not a criteria?"

He watched her withdrawn and weary expression.

"I have my reasons," she answered, her voice barely above a whisper. "Reasons that I don't care to discuss. What I do now is much more important than my playing or performing for a room full of people. What I'm trying to do could change the lives of millions," she added, almost as if she tried to justify what she was doing, Clay thought.

"I didn't mean to pry. We all do what we have to do."

She nodded. "I'm glad you understand."

He wasn't sure that he did, but one thing was certain, she was hiding something. Whatever it was, as long as it didn't interfere with what he was hired to do, it was fine with him, he supposed.

"One more thing," Clay said. "Since we're going to be working together, would you call me Clay?"

She laughed. It was a soft, tinkling sound. "My friends call me Dee. And," she added with a devilish smile, "they don't move my furniture around."

"Touché."

CHAPTER VI

Deanna walked with Clay to the door, and although they'd spent several hours talking, he didn't want to leave her. It was a strange sensation to him. It had been so long since he'd been in the company of a woman from whom he didn't want to escape as quickly as possible. Deanna was totally different, and that difference intrigued him.

He stood in the open doorway, virtually shuffling his feet, trying to find the perfect one-liner that would prolong their evening.

"It's a beautiful night...it seems," she said, a wistful note in her voice. Her head titled upward as if she was trying to envision the cloudless heaven, or conjure up images of the past.

"Yes...it is." He suddenly wanted to kiss her, trail his mouth along the smooth column of her long neck. He shook his head, scattering the vision to find her appearing to look at him, a soft smile on her lips, a sense of poignant pause in her body as if she was waiting...

"Would you like to go for a walk?" he blurted out.

Deanna blinked rapidly as if startled out of a dream. Her hands rose to her throat. "I don't..."

"Go for walks?"

"No. Of course. I mean I don't think it would be a good idea."

"For two business associates to take a stroll on a beautiful summer evening?"

He could see her pulling herself together, a response framing in her mind.

"I can't."

The tone was so sharp, so final, it felt as if he'd been slapped, causing him to involuntarily step back, and he could have sworn he saw panic dart across her face.

"No problem. Just a suggestion." He balled his hands into fists to keep from reaching out and stroking the worried look from her face.

She gripped the doorknob. "I really should be going in."

"Right."

"We'll talk again. Soon. I'll have my associate Tracy Moore give you a call so that the two of you can meet. She's also the Foundation's attorney."

"Fine." He turned and started down the steps, then over his shoulder he said, "Good night."

He thought he heard a soft response, but he couldn't be sure. What he did hear was the click of the locks as the door was shut behind him.

If he'd slept five minutes the entire night, he'd slept a long time. His night was filled with images of Deanna, the soft angles of her face, the husky whisper of her voice, the sound of her open laughter, her intellectual acumen. Packaged all together, she was irresistible, except for the wall that she'd constructed around herself, a protective fortress.

He might not be the most sensitive man in the world, but he generally had a good handle on people, except when it came to Deanna Winters. She'd already shot holes in his everyone-is-trying-to-get-over theory. Barring that, he still believed that she was standing behind a wall, and that the kind, witty, benevolent, talented persona she projected to the world only scratched the surface.

He rolled over in the king-size bed and peeked at the digital clock through bleary, sleep-deprived eyes. Ten o'clock A.M. Maybe if he just lay there a little longer sleep would come.

Instead, the phone rang, and he cursed. He started to let the machine take the call but figured he'd have to call the person back anyway. On the third ring, he picked up the phone.

"Hello?"

"Mr. McDaniels, this is Tracy Moore, Deanna's associate."

Clay rubbed his eyes and slowly sat up. "Yes. Good morning." He cleared his throat.

"I'm sorry to call you at home, but I tried your office and was told you wouldn't be in until later. Deanna gave me your home number."

"No problem. She said we should meet."

"That's why I'm calling. I was hoping we could do that today."

This one didn't let any grass grow under her feet, he mused. "Lunch would work for me. Say about noon," he stated more than asked. Couldn't let her start off thinking he could be dictated to, but he could also be magnanimous. "You pick the place and I'll meet you."

"How about B. Smith's on—"

"Sounds perfect. I know just where it is."

"Great. So I'll see you at noon."

"Oh, how will I know?"

Tracy laughed. "Don't worry, I'll know you. Deanna gives great descriptions."

Clay sat on the edge of the bed for several moments with the dial tone humming in his ear. Tracy's last statement left him completely bewildered. Obviously she was joking. She had to be. His own stupidity had proven that Deanna couldn't see. So how could she give a description of him to someone else?

No, he was awake, and noon couldn't come fast enough.

Clay arrived at the restaurant ten minutes early, but wound up being ten minutes late getting inside after having to hunt down a parking space. It was the one thing that made a personal hell out of living in New York.

He pushed down his annoyance as he opened the glass doors of the restaurant and hoped that the efficient Ms. Moore wouldn't look too unfavorably on his tardiness. Strolling over to the reception podium, he looked over heads and scanned the semi-darkened interior.

"Welcome to B. Smith's. May I help you?" asked the hostess, demurely clad in black and white.

"I'm meeting someone," he responded, glancing briefly at her, then back across the sea of tables. "But thanks anyway."

He gave her a short smile, then shot his cuffs to check the time. Twelve-fifteen. Hmm. *This is worse than a blind date.*

"Hi. I'm Tracy Moore."

Clay turned to look down into the sparkling brown eyes of an extremely attractive woman. Though short by his standards, she was definitely packaged well. Her tailored magenta suit outlined her body like an artist's stroke, with the skirt hitting just above the knees to showcase a great pair of legs.

He blinked and realized that she was holding out her hand, which he quickly shook, finding her grip surprisingly strong and assertive for someone so small.

"Obviously you know who I am," he quipped. "Did my looking around like a tourist tip you off?"

Tracy grinned. She gave him a quick once over. He was glad he'd chosen his midnight-blue suit and hand-painted silk tie. Both brought him luck, and he had a feeling he'd need it with Ms. Moore. Despite the grin, she seemed all business.

"Actually, it was Deanna's description. She was on the mark, as usual. It's a little game we play," she added in conspiratorial tone.

"Oh. I see." But he didn't. "You want to tell me how that works?"

"Maybe over lunch. I'm starved."

Between bites of grilled chicken, baked potatoes, and seasoned-to-perfection green beans, Clay was given clear details as to his responsibilities for the Deanna Winters

Foundation and became privy to a world that few were allowed to enter.

"After the accident, Deanna was a mess in every sense of the word. She wouldn't talk to anyone. She refused therapy. She wouldn't play the piano, and riding again was out of the question. She just shut herself off from the world." Tracy took a breath. "I was afraid for her."

"What finally turned her around? She certainly isn't that person anymore." He took a bite of his chicken.

"Strangely enough it was Cord Herrera."

Clay frowned in surprise. Since he'd been hired by Deanna he'd had Grace pull every single article, photo, and gossip column that she could find on Deanna. According to everything he'd read, the romance between the movie idol and the musician was hot and heavy, fraught with stories of other women and Cord's fiery temper. Knowing what little he did about Deanna, he was hard-pressed to imagine her and Cord together in the first place.

"Herrera?" he asked. "He doesn't come across as the compassionate type. If what I read is true, the cold-hearted bastard dumped her after the accident."

Tracy took a slow sip of wine. "I really don't know if I should be telling you this," she began, seeming to measure her words. "But maybe it will help you to understand Deanna better since the two of you will have to work very closely together."

Clay leaned back in his seat and waited.

"Cord didn't actually leave her because of, or after, the accident. Their relationship was beginning to unravel before then, for a variety of reasons, which I won't get into. The truth is, Deanna finally left him."

Her eyes took on a faraway look as she continued to talk.

"Deanna had a difficult childhood. As a child prodigy, she was always engulfed in lessons and recitals, practice, practice. Her one outlet was her riding. She loved to ride as much as she loved to play the piano—maybe even more so. As a result, she never made real friends, or was involved in relationships. Her parents—if you want to call them that— never allowed her to enter the real world, deal with problems, make her own decisions.

"Sure, she traveled extensively, was photographed constantly, she performed for royalty, but she never had a life. And as much as I hate to admit it, not until she met Cord the night she won her first Grammy."

"In other words, Cord showed her the real world?" His tolerance for suspension of disbelief had reached its limits, but he held his skeptical tongue.

"Or at least a world she'd never been a part of before." Tracy leaned slightly forward. "Deanna began to cling to Cord, depend on him. So much so that, for fear of losing her lifeline, she ignored his indiscretions."

Clay's male protective instincts went on full alert. "What are you saying—exactly?" he hissed under his breath, his eyes darting quickly around the restaurant for potential eavesdroppers.

Tracy lowered her gaze and appeared to be seriously considering how much more she could safely say. They she looked up, directly into his eyes.

"Let's just say that, good or bad, Cord visited her after the accident and saw the shell of the person she'd become. I think even he was devastated. And in his own inimitable style challenged her to be either a pitiful burden on society or the real woman who'd finally stood up to him. He walked out of that hospital room, and they haven't seen or spoken to each other since."

She let out a long breath. "I'm telling you this because I get a very strong vibe from you. An honest vibe, decent. I've gotten the same thing from Dee. She told me what happened when the two of you met. And she also told me why she still wants to work with you." She put her arms on the table and leaned closer. "Deanna is like a sister to me."

Her eyes bored into his, and he had the unsettling feeling that this petite woman would snatch his heart out if he hurt Deanna again.

"I've seen her stripped down to her naked soul and, layer by layer, rebuild herself from the inside out. She's been hurt, used, and unloved for most of her life, but she's a survivor. I just don't want to have to see her survive any more tragedies, physical or emotional."

There was no mistaking the barely veiled threat. She'd cut him off at the knees if he did anything to hurt her friend. The reality was, she could do it. With the connections the Foundation had, all it would take was one phone call. Deanna, he believed, didn't have that kind of ruthless nature. Tracy Moore, however, was a different story. And he liked her. She had heart.

"You love her a lot, don't you?"

She gave him a tight smile and a slow nod. "You're the first man in years that she's allowing to be in direct contact with her. She may be a renowned musician, a philanthropist, and a phenomenal businesswoman, but she has a soft heart and a need to be loved. That makes her vulnerable."

Her meaning was crystal clear. Clay said, "I wouldn't do anything to compromise myself or her."

"I'm so glad to hear that." She finished off her chicken, then daintily wiped her mouth. She smiled brightly. "Now that we have those issues out of the way, do you have any questions about your role and our expectations?"

"Not at the moment."

"Good." She signaled for the check. "My treat." She placed her platinum American Express on the table. "I'll have the contract drawn up and sent to your office in the morning."

"Fine." He deposited his linen napkin next to his plate.

The waiter returned with her credit card and the bill for her signature.

"It was a pleasure meeting you, Clay."

"You as well. I'm sure this arrangement will work out just fine."

She rose to leave.

"How did you recognize me, Tracy? You never told me. You can't leave me hanging."

She grinned, slinging her bag over her shoulder. She placed her hand on her hip and tilted her head to the side. "She said you're about six feet two because of the height that your voice projects over her head. And that you'd have a strong build. She could tell when you kept her from falling. She told me to look for strong, large hands and close-cropped soft but curly hair."

Clay frowned in confusion at that one.

Tracy laughed. "Your hair apparently brushed against her cheek. And she said you've have a dark brown complexion. She said she could tell by the warmth of your skin when she held your hand. And, 'he sounds like a preacher.' Her exact words. And if all that fails, he wears Air by Michael Jordan." She flashed him a grin. "Is she good or what?"

Clay shook his head in amazement. "Good is an understatement. Does she read minds, too?"

"Hey, you never know. She's forced herself to develop her sensorial skills until they're honed to razor sharpness. She's had no choice. It's been her way to recovery since the accident. It's almost been her substitute for reentering life.

Tracy gave him a half smile. "So be careful what you think."

They walked to the exit and stood facing each other on the sidewalk.

"Can I give you a lift somewhere, Tracy? My car is parked around the corner."

"No. I'm fine. Thanks. I'm going to take a cab over to Deanna's. We have some business to discuss, and I want to bring her up to date on our meeting."

"If you're sure it's no problem." Taking Tracy would be an excuse to see Deanna again.

"Don't worry about it. Anything you want me to tell her?" She angled her head and arched a thin brow.

He got the distinct impression that she wanted him to reveal something—maybe his feelings or impressions about Deanna, which he wasn't quite sure what they were.

"Just let her know that I'm truly impressed with her deductive skills. But what's going to happen if I change my cologne?"

Tracy laughed and stuck out her hand, which Clay shook. "I'll be sure to tell her. Talk with you again next week." She turned and walked away.

"And Tracy," he called out.

She slowed but didn't stop, looking over her shoulder.

"Tell her that I'm really looking forward to working with her."

She gave him a smile and a wave, then ducked inside a yellow cab, which had screeched to a halt.

Clay proceed in the opposite direction, toward his car. He was looking forward to seeing Deanna again, being in her company. There was something about her that had pricked open the seal around his emotions. He stopped on the corner for a red light, wondering how he was going to maintain a safe distance from her. He'd think that with her inability to see, it would be an automatic barrier to his feelings. It wasn't. If anything, it seemed to make her even more intriguing.

CHAPTER VII

When Clay walked into his office later that afternoon, Grace was seated at his desk as if she belonged there.

"Well, good afternoon, Boss Man," she greeted in a tone that sounded as if she paid the bills.

Clay dropped his briefcase into an antique wing chair—a gift from a grateful client—then strode to the left side of the room to the small but well-stocked bar and poured a glass of seltzer over ice. He took a long swallow, turned, and shot Grace a dark scowl, which, of course, didn't faze her.

"You wanna get out of my chair now?"

Grace twisted her lips and slowly rose, only to rest her ample hips on the edge of his desk. "I'll just cut to the chase. What's Ms. Moore like, and how was the meeting?"

Clay took his sweet time sitting down. He made a show of drinking his seltzer. If he knew anyone, he knew Grace and her thirst for information. Holding back was the only way he could ever keep her in check. So he took his time.

"Any messages?" He sifted through the mail on his desk, carefully avoiding her gaze.

"Oh, it's gonna be like that, huh? No problem. Then I guess I won't tell you about the message I got from Ms. Winters not more than twenty minutes ago." With that she hopped down from the desk edge and sashayed toward the door.

"Freeze."

"You rang?" she singsonged, completing a smooth pirouette.

"What's the message, Gracie?"

"Will you tell me how your meeting went?"

"Don't I always?" he tossed back, struggling to contain the rush of eagerness.

"Okay, then." Grace flashed him a bright-white smile. "She said if you're free this evening, about eight, she'd appreciate it if you would stop by."

His heart knocked. "Did she say why?"

"Nope. Just to give her a call one way or the other."

Clay nodded. His thoughts running off in a million different directions. He cleared his throat. "Call her and tell her I'll be there."

"I already did."

Clay shook his head. "One of these days, Alice, bang, zoom, right in the kisser!"

"You can tell me about your meeting later. Some of us have real work to do." Opening the door, Grace looked at him over her shoulder. Her eyes held all the warmth and the secrets they had shared. "Have a good time tonight, Clay. I mean that."

Every iota clothing was put together with infinite care. Standing in front of his full-length mirror, Clay adjusted his pearl-gray tie set and a silk shirt of the same hue. His double-breasted suit, a mix of rayon and silk in a darker shade of gray, had been made for him during one of his trips to Japan. Satisfied, he looked on top of his dresser, which showcased an array of fragrances. He smiled, picked up the distinctive bottle of Air and dabbed it on his cheeks.

Clay McDaniels…looking good. Feeling good.

Until he parked a few doors from Deanna's house. When he trotted up the steps and rang the bell, he realized his palms were damp.

He muttered a curse, snatched a handkerchief from the breast pocket of his jacket and briskly wiped his hands just as the door was pulled open.

"Hello, Clay."

Her smile ignited a tiny flame in the pit of his stomach. She stood framed in the doorway, a halo of soft light from the foyer surrounding her. Music from somewhere in the house floated in the twilight. Dark hair glistened against bare shoulders, the rippling waves reminding him of the ocean's gentle undulations. She wore a pale peach sundress in a near-sheer gauze fabric that fell from the soft rise of her breasts to just above her slender ankles.

Her look was totally feminine, lethally seductive.

He moved to the top step, catching the subtle scent of soap and the barest hint of perfume and swallowed the impulse to kiss her, just once to see what it was like. Instead, he said, "I didn't think we'd have the chance to meet again so soon."

"I hope it's not a problem."

"Of course not." He hesitated a beat. "I'm glad you called."

Something quick, hot, and dark flashed across her face and then was gone. Her breasts rose and fell just a bit quicker. He could feel her heat, or was it his?

"Please…come in."

Clay stepped across the threshold, but Deanna didn't move back quite far enough and his arm grazed her breasts.

He thought he heard her sharp intake of breath in concert with the instantaneous rush that throbbed between his thighs. But it could have been just the pulse pounding in his ears. *This is going to be a long night.*

"I hope you haven't eaten dinner yet. I fixed something light to munch on while we talk."

"Sounds fine. If it's anything like the breakfast you put out, I'm game."

Deanna laughed, that soft musical laugh that just made you feel good.

"Nothing quite that elaborate, I'm afraid. But I think you'll enjoy it. We can eat in the living room. I thought we'd be more comfortable."

More comfortable. What did she mean by that?

Clay followed her into the living area, which he took a moment to notice this time. The rectangle-shape room had an airy outdoor feel to it. Plants, none of which he could name, sprouted from every available space. The furnishings were strictly modern. But peach was obviously her favorite color. The modular leather couch, matching love seat, the infamous ottoman, and throw pillows in all sizes and shapes were of the same easy-on-the-eye hue. Off in the corner stood a magnificent black grand piano that glistened with a vibrancy of its own, seeming to beckon you to hear it tell its story. But what gave the room the ultimate touch of class was the gleaming wood floor reflecting all that graced it.

Beyond those touches and the cherrywood coffee and end tables, and what appeared to be a six-foot-long antique server set against the far wall, the room was bare. There were no photographs, no picture on the wall, no magazines, no personal memorabilia. Yet it still felt warm and lived in.

"I hope you like grilled salmon," Deanna said, easing her way into his survey.

His gaze zeroed in on her. She looked perfect here, as if this was where she belonged—in a beautiful castle away from the harsh realities of life. And then the full gravity of his thought began to take on a new dimension.

Was the world she had once faced too harsh? Was that why she'd retreated and created her own—one in which she was in control? He wanted to ask her. A part of him needed to know. He'd have to find the right time.

"You don't like it? Salmon."

Her voice snapped him back into focus. "Oh, I'm sorry. Yes. I do." He chuckled to hide his embarrassment. "I was checking out the room. It says a lot about you."

Her face flushed. "What does it tell you?"

"That you like the feeling of open space, quality furnishing, but not an abundance of them. The room is totally feminine without being frilly. Your home is your sanctuary."

She was quiet.

"This room is personal in a way. There's nothing here that reflects anything that the owner may think or feel, but just like you, it's self-contained. And peach is your favorite color."

"You're very intuitive, Clay. It must serve you well in your work."

He smiled. "Most of the time."

"Meaning?"

"Sometimes I can't quite put my finger on a particular client. What their real agenda is sometimes escapes me."

"Anyone in particular?" She moved easily toward the server and lifted a plate.

"You."

She turned toward him and blinked as if she could somehow get him into focus, then turned back toward the server.

"Help yourself," she offered, seemingly not intending to respond to his comment, which to Clay was more telling than anything she could have said.

"Your first assignment, Mr. McDaniels, is to pick up a very sizable donation from a Mrs. Donovan in London." Deanna took a sip of wine. "She has a cashier's check for one hundred and fifty thousand dollars, which she wants to give to the Institute, which is just getting underway. Her grand-daughter was born blind, so Mrs. Donovan is very sensitive to the issues and wants to give us all the support she can."

"When do you need me to be there?"

"Well...I know you haven't seen the contract yet. And it may have been presumptuous of me to schedule you to meet with her...Friday. But I did it anyway."

"Friday? You do realize that you're not my only client," he said, his voice light with incredulity. "If this is going to work we'll have to coordinate a lot better."

"I know, and I apologize. I was just so excited when I got the call. I—"

"Don't worry about it. Consider it done." He leaned back in his seat. "The only person I worry about is Grace. She goes ballistic when she's not in total control of my itinerary."

"She's certainly a character. I got that from our conversations." Deanna paused. "She thinks a lot of you."

"It's mutual. She's been with me from the days when I was running my messenger service." And through my divorce, a string of women, and my bouts of depression, he thought but didn't say. He took a sip of wine. "Anyway, you can get directly in contact with Grace. She knows more about what I'm doing than me."

He thought he saw the slightest bit of regret dance across her face, her animated features dulling briefly. Why? And then, in an instant, it hit him. She wanted to be able to deal with him directly. Maybe it was his male ego talking, but somehow he didn't think so. Her follow-up smile seemed forced, or so he thought.

"So what did you think of Tracy, my 'better half,' as she calls herself?" Deanna asked.

"She's certainly focused, very business minded, funny, smart. And she cares a great deal about you." He thought about the things Tracy had revealed to him and wondered if Deanna would ever be that open with him.

"Tracy and I go back more years than I can count." She smiled a faraway smile. "Every triumph. Every heartache. She's been there to either cheer me on or tell me to get up off my butt and try again."

"Did she ever tell you to play again?" he asked gently.

The room suddenly became very still. Even the soft music that had kept them company all evening seemed to cease, awaiting her answer.

After a lengthy pause she simply stated, "Yes."

"And?"

She folded her hands in her lap. "It was the one thing she failed at."

"Tracy doesn't seem like the type of person who gives up easily."

"She isn't. It's an ongoing battle between us. She insists. I say no."

Clay leaned forward. "Would you ever play for a private audience of one?"

She blinked rapidly, pressing her lips together as if she were trying to form the words to answer, realizing what he was asking. "I don't think so."

"Why, Deanna?"

"I don't…play anymore."

"You're so self-reliant, determined, centered on your goals. Why are you afraid of something that you're so incredibly good at?"

The glass of wine wobbled slightly in her hand. "Who says I'm afraid? My life…is different now. It has been for five years. Playing for an audience of one or one million isn't going to change that."

"It might change it for you," he said gently.

Her chin jutted defiantly. "Why do you care?"

"Honestly?"

"Yes. Honestly."

"Because from the little I've seen and what I've heard from someone very close to you, you're worth caring about. The world misses your music, your playing. They miss the magic spells that you cast over their lives. I know I do."

She lowered her head. "You don't understand."

"No, I don't. So *tell* me."

She expelled a long breath. "Maybe some other time."

"I'm going to hold you to that." He placed his glass on the end table, then stood. "I hate to leave, but I have a meeting in the morning."

Deanna rose.

"Dinner was wonderful. One day maybe you'll tell me how you manage it all."

She smiled. "Now that's a promise."

They walked down the corridor and into the foyer.

"I still think you have little elves running around in your kitchen."

Deanna giggled. "Close, but no cigars. Months and months of ruthless training by a culinary therapist who didn't have a compassionate bone in his body is more like it."

Clay turned toward her as they stood in the doorway. His voice dropped to an intimate low. "He did a fabulous job." He wanted to touch her, run his hands across her face. Felt her breath rush against his mouth the instant before he kissed her.

Suddenly his early morning meeting was no longer important. He didn't want the evening to end. Not yet.

"There was just one thing missing from the evening," he said, fighting down his raging hormones.

Her slender hands fluttered to her exposed neck. "What? I thought—"

"Dessert."

Her expression visibly relaxed. The lines of monetary tension around her eyes and mouth eased. "Oops."

"That can easily be rectified. You can accompany me to Baskin Robbins. I have a strong craving for butter pecan ice cream."

"Oh…no…I couldn't."

"You don't eat ice cream?"

"Yes, but—"

"It's a beautiful night. The store is only a block away. And, honestly, I want to spend some more time with you."

"What?"

"You may not be able to *see*, Ms. Winters, but I know your hearing is working just fine."

"But—"

"I can be just as determined and as stubborn as you. I won't take no for an answer this time." He plucked the key that hung from a hook by the door, took her arm, and gently led her out. "You cheated me out of a private concert, but I have to put my foot down when it comes to dessert."

He tucked her hand securely in the crook of his arm, closed the door, and led her down the stairs.

He felt her whole body tense, tiny tremors running through her slender frame. She's terrified, he realized, now second-guessing his hasty decision. Maybe he should just take her back inside.

"I can hardly recall the last time I actually walked along the streets of Manhattan," she said, almost to herself.

He looked down at her, and she was biting her bottom lip.

"How do you get groceries? Clothes?"

"I have everything delivered. What I don't order by phone, Tracy takes care of."

She was breathing harder now, as if she were stepping into the throes of a panic attack.

"Do you want to go back, Deanna?"

"No." Her hand tightened on his arm. "I…think I need to do this."

He gazed at her, so delicate, so vulnerable, so very strong. His heart seemed to knot in his chest as a rush of warm emotion flooded him. "What kind of ice cream do you like?"

Deanna grinned. "Pistachio."

By the time they returned to Deanna's house, she had calmed considerably, holding up her end of the light, nonthreatening conversation. She laughed at his jokes and his often racy descriptions of passerby whispered in her ear. Several times she nudged him the ribs for talking too loud about a trio of girls, who, according to Clay, were dead ringers for Elvira.

"Here you are safe, and sound," he announced in front of her building. He walked her up the steps and opened the door.

She turned to him in the frame of the doorway. Her smile was soft, almost angelic. "Thank you. I had a wonderful evening and an awakening experience."

He reached out, a single finger extended, and touched the corner of her mouth. "Ice cream."

He thought she would blush, or at the very least pull back. Instead she reached for his face, slowly, tentatively, with both hands until they rested on his jaws. Her eyes closed.

Like a sculptor checking her creation, she traced with gentle fingers the planes of his face, seeming to commit each arch, curve, and indentation to memory. His entire body became infused with a white-hot heat, which she continued to stroke with each gentler caress. It was one of the most sensual experiences he'd ever been through. It took every ounce of will power to keep from pulling her into his arms, see what she felt like pressed against him.

"Just as I thought," she said in a hushed voice. "Your family has strong African genes. It's in the sharpness of your cheekbones." Her fingers grazed them, and his stomach muscles clenched. Her thumbs traced the outline of his lips. "Full," she whispered, and he felt a shudder ripple down his spine.

Her fingers splayed across his forehead searching the arch of his brow, the slope of his eyes. "You'd be considered quite handsome by most," she said in a thoughtful voice, slowly removing her hands. "My thoughts of you were very close."

He could scarcely speak. "Were they?"

"Yes." She stepped back and braced her hand against the door frame. "I hope you don't mind. I should have asked."

"No. It's all right. Really. It was—" He inhaled. "Different." His gaze wandered over her face, her form. "I want to kiss you," he suddenly said, the overwhelming desire to voice his need overshadowing common sense. "Say yes and let it happen. Tell me no and I'll be on my way."

"Yes." Her hand reached for his face. "Yes."

His heart hammered in his chest, so loud it drowned out the sounds of the night. He stepped up to her, cupped her chin in his palm, then lowered his head until his mouth touched hers. He inhaled her soft sigh. He breathed her in like a life-giving force, the warmth emitted from her gliding through his veins.

He pressed closer his fingers caressing her cheek, tangling in her hair. His tongue flicked tentatively across her lips, then with more urgency when she offered no resistance.

She seemed to welcome him, hesitantly at first, but then with gentle abandon.

Their tongues danced a leisurely mating dance, taking their time to explore, to savor. His hands slid down her neck, along the column of her back. He moaned ever so slightly when he felt the hardened tips of her breasts brush against his chest.

Deanna's answering sighs were soft, almost soundless at first, and then they began to build to shuddering whimpers. His mouth left hers to explore the soft sweetness of her neck. He felt her body tense as she began to mumble incoherently. At first he thought her whispered cries of "please" meant that she wanted more of him, until he realized she was struggling, her hand digging into her back, and her cries growing stronger, almost frantic.

He let her go.

"Please…don't hurt me," she cried. "Don't hurt me."

Terrified, Clay pulled back, his first thought was that he'd been set up and she was going to cry rape. But when he looked into her face and saw a fear so pervasive, he knew this was no ploy. This was real, and Deanna was frightened to death.

Cautiously he gathered her into his arms, uttering soothing sounds into her ear while he gently stroked her hair.

Her entire body trembled as if she'd been left outside in the elements in the dead of winter.

"It's all right, Dee. I won't hurt you. I promise. Sssh, don't cry. Please don't cry."

She took short, gasping breaths. "I'm sorry. Clay, I—"

"Sssh. Come on, let me take you inside." He wrapped an arm around her shoulder, pulling most of her weight toward him, and led her into the house.

Once she was curled up on the couch, Clay sat opposite her on a love seat, a bit reluctant to get too close for fear of igniting another scene. Something had spooked her. There was no question about that. And whatever it was didn't start with him. That much he was sure of, but not much else.

He watched her as she huddled on the couch, head turned away from him, her face hidden behind the tumble of thick hair. "Can I get you anything? Some tea, wine?"

She wouldn't raise her head in his direction when she finally spoke. "I feel like such a fool. I don't know what happened," she said in a halting voice, almost talking to herself. "I'm so sorry." Her voice cracked. "I guess you must think I'm some sort of nutcase."

"It's all right, Deanna. Really. I shouldn't have put you in that position. It was out of line."

She finally raised her head, tilting it in the direction of his voice and with her uncanny ability to appear focused, "looked" at him. "Was I out of line for...saying yes, for responding?"

"No, but I shouldn't—" Now he felt like a babbling idiot when all he wanted to do was take her back in his arms and keep her ghosts away. "Do you want to talk about it?"

She shook her head. "I...can't."

"Would it be okay if I sat next to you for a minute? I promise I won't touch you."

Slowly she nodded, and he sat beside her, keeping a reasonable distance. He took a deep breath, trying to organize his swirling thoughts into something that made sense.

"Listen, I'm not sure what's happening between us. But I know it's something, and I know you feel it too. It has nothing to do with business, which makes it complicated. Stop me when I'm saying something wrong." He waited, then started again. "I'm an emotional wreck myself. My divorce did a real number on me." He couldn't tell her the worst of it. The part that he still couldn't handle.

She reached out and found his hand and held it.

"It's been a few years, but it's still hard for me to trust a woman. Or myself. I guess I convinced myself that I'd never get myself involved in another relationship that had the possibility of hurting me like that again." He swallowed and dared to lean a bit closer. "Until I met you."

He saw the quick intake of breath, the slight widening of her eyes, the soft flush that rushed to her face, and he was certain that she was going to tell him to get out. His heart raced as the seconds ticked.

"I know this is sudden." He clutched for something, anything that would keep her from turning him away. "I'm willing to wait. To back off. Whatever."

"Clay." She reached out and found his cheek and gently cupped it in her hand. "I'm not like...other women. I can't sit with you and watch a movie, see a play, read a newspaper, watch the sun rise or set. I can't...even see your...face."

Shimmering pools formed in her eyes, but it seemed that by sheer will she pulled the tears aback. "Why would you want me?"

He knew that everything hinged on his answer. Her question was only candy coating for what she really wanted to know.

"Deanna." He took her hand and held it. "Everything that you ever were, all that you are and what you can still become, makes me want to be with you. Your laughter, your brains, your courage, your beauty, and your compassion are all qualities than any man would want. I know I do."

"But you don't even know me," she protested.

"What I do know makes me want to know more."

She sat there for several moments, and all Clay could hear was the pulse drumming in his ears. He couldn't remember the last time he wanted anything as much as he wanted her to say, "Yes, we'll work it out."

"There's so much about me that you don't know, Clay. Things I don't even understand about myself. I don't know if I'm ready for a relationship, or when I'll ever be."

His spirits dropped to ground zero. "That's fine, Dee. I didn't mean to push you. I shouldn't have kissed you. I suppose I let my own wants overshadow was the right thing to do. I'm sorry."

"Please don't apologize. I...enjoyed it."

"You did? Then why are you so hesitant? I don't understand."

"Neither do I. At least not yet. It's been a long time for me...with anyone." She swallowed. "I can't ask you to wait until I figure it all out."

"Why not?"

"It wouldn't be fair to you."

"Why don't you let me decide what's fair for me? Fair enough?"

She smiled, shy and sweet. "I can't make any promises, Clay."

"I'm not asking for any."

To him it seemed that she was taking a tentative step in the dark, seeking out a corner of her heart, searching for the light.

"I might have a taste for some ice cream one night soon," she whispered.

And so it began.

CHAPTER VIII

In the ensuing weeks, Clay's every waking hour was consumed with work and travel. He and Deanna spent brief but quality-building time together, really getting to know each other, in business and out, at least when his schedule allowed. In one week alone, he'd been to Chicago, Boston, and San Diego, making deals, transporting merchandise and huge sums of money. Through it all, his thoughts barely strayed from Deanna. He was still shaken by the scene with her. The possibilities of what had terrified her only served to fuel his imagination with awful visions. She had yet to tell him what had happened. Had she been raped, abused? Was she afraid that her lack of vision would hamper or spoil a relationship? What was it?

But she'd said, "don't hurt me." Someone had, and the idea tortured him. How could anyone have hurt her to the point that she was afraid of intimacy with a man? She'd been engaged to Cord Herrera. He couldn't imagine that they didn't have...*Cord?*

Anger, rage, boiled like an erupting volcano in his belly. He shut his eyes, pushing back his own emotions and tried to focus on what Deanna must be dealing with and had gone through.

He'd have to be gentle with her, patient, get her to trust him, to trust herself. He'd take as much time as she needed, as long as she was willing to try.

He wondered what she was doing, what she was wearing, was she happy, did she want to see him again as much as he wanted to see her? It had taken all of his self-control to keep from calling her as he stared up at the endless string of ceiling in his empty hotel rooms, wishing for the next day that would bring him closer to the end of the week—to home and to her. He needed to be sure that whatever decision she made was made because it was what she wanted.

Although he might be jumping the gun just a little, on the flight home he wondered what type of life they could possibly have together. Ninety percent of his time was spent in the air and in strange rooms. Would Deanna be willing to travel again? Although she was strong and resilient, she had quite a fear of the outside world. Tracy had said as much, and he'd witnessed it himself. Deanna had created total insulation, functioning in the areas that she'd mastered. Her entire life had been based on her abilities and other people's opinions of her. He wanted to be the one to make her understand things differently, if she'd let him.

What was wrong with him? It seemed as though he'd become consumed by thoughts of her, which grew more intense as the days progressed. If this was how he felt now, how would he feel when he took the next step? The prospect shook him.

The "fasten your seat belt" sign flashed, and a wave of anticipation filled him. Before the day was over he was going to make it a point to see her. He wanted to broaden her horizons, help her cross the line again. Why, he wasn't sure. Maybe for once in his life he could make a difference that would count for something.

As usual, his first stop was the office and, as usual, it was full of activity.

"Welcome back, Boss Man." Grace followed him into his office, closing the door behind her.

Clay dropped his bags next to the desk and turned to face her. "Wassup? Bring me up to date." He began to sort through the mound of mail.

"The account with Mr. Weinstein in the diamond district is set. Jason is taking care of the shipment to Israel next week."

"Great. What else?" He tossed a letter on the desk and looked at the next one.

"We got a call from Sotheby's, the auction house. It has some antiques that it needs delivered to Brazil for some diplomat. It seems it's not too pleased with the service it's been using, and you were recommended by one of its clients."

Clay loosened his tie, running a finger around his neck before shrugging out of his jacket.

Grace paused and slipped her glasses off the bridge of her nose. "That's the end of the good news."

Clay looked up from the mail.

"Rachael called. She's in town and wants to see you. She left a number."

"Don't bother giving it to me," he ground out, when the initial shock of hearing his ex-wife's name had worn off. "I won't be using it."

Grace gave him a long look from beneath mascaraed lashes. "She said it's about your son. About Matthew."

The bottom dropped out of his world.

CHAPTER IX

From the moment the judge had decreed the divorce final and awarded sole custody of their year-old son to Rachael, the only way Clay could make himself go on was by blocking Matthew out. Rachael had taken him, remarried, and moved to Chicago. Most of Clay's attempts to see his son were rebuffed. But still he made child support payments like clockwork, sent gifts and cards at all the appropriate times while keeping a seal on his heart.

Finally Clay found his voice. "What did she say...about Matt?"

"She said he wants to see you, and there are other things she needs to discuss with you," Grace said gently.

Clay turned away, not daring to face her with the look of pain that must be carved on his face. "Just leave the number on my desk." He slung his hands in his pockets and moved slowly toward the window. "I'll get to it," he mumbled.

Hours later he still hadn't called. He'd gone home, showered, changed, unpacked his bags, and had two glasses of wine. Still he couldn't make his fingers dial the number.

What did Rachael want? Why did Matthew want to see him now, after all this time? Or was it just one of Rachael's schemes? And where was her business tycoon husband in all this?

How something that was once so beautiful could have gone so wrong still bewildered him.

Rachael. Homecoming queen. Rachael, most likely to succeed. Rachael, the woman who gave grown men wet dreams. Rachael, the one who nearly destroyed him.

He tossed back the last of the wine and started to pour another when he stopped midway, realizing what he was doing, stalling for time.

He looked at the slip of paper with Rachael's number in Grace's elegant handwriting. Taking a deep breath of resolve, he picked up the paper and the phone next to the bar and dialed.

The phone rang three times, and just as he was about to hang up, Rachael's voice came across the line.

"It's me. Clay. I got a message that you called." His head began to pound.

"Hello, Clay. You could sound a little happier."

The soft, sexy voice that had once driven him wild with need now grated on his nerves like nails scratching against a blackboard.

"What is it, Rachael? You told Grace it was about Matthew."

"I want you to see him." She exhaled on what sounded like a long, exasperated breath.

"You've done everything in your power to keep me away from my son since the day our divorce was final. Why now, Rachael?"

"I didn't realize I needed to have a reason for you to see your son."

"You have a reason for everything."

"Don't, Clay. It's pointless. This is a courtesy call."

"Then let me courteously tell you to get to the point."

There was a long moment of silence before she finally responded. "We're moving back to New York...and I want you to take an active role in our son's life."

He felt his insides shift, something in him opened up, and the air caught in his throat. How many nights had he wished, prayed for this day? Now here she was, handing him back his son on a silver platter. But why couldn't he trust her? His heart hammered.

"So where is hubby in this picture?" he forced himself to ask.

"Steven won't be coming."

That revelation jolted him. He swallowed back the knot in his throat. "When can I see Matt?"

He hung up after making a date to see Matthew on Sunday. Rachael would bring him to his house, the one they all once shared. How ironic.

Lying across his bed, Clay went over the conversation with Rachael. Even after all this time she still had the uncanny ability to turn him inside out and upside down. But the idea of seeing his son again gave him back his equilibrium. What would he say to his son? How would Matthew react? Did Matt even know him anymore?

He'd drive himself crazy if he kept going like this, and he knew there was no way he could get any work done or get any sleep. He needed to talk. He didn't want to be alone.

Then it hit him. He didn't have anyone he could just talk with or hang out with. Except for Grace. But he was strangely reluctant to call her. She was good as an office manager, and a good friend who had stood by him in tough times. But right now he needed something more. Something different. But he didn't have any other friends because he had allowed his job and his drive for success to consume him. He'd had to in order to mentally and emotionally survive the destruction of his marriage and his family. Now the business was all he had. That and the possibility of rekindling his relationship with his son.

The phone rang, jarring him from this dark musings. His first thought was that it was Rachael calling back to say she'd changed her mind, as she'd done on so many other occasions.

With a great deal of reluctance, he answered the phone.

"Clay. It's Deanna. I hope I'm not disturbing you."

He sat up, and a smile drifted across his face and into his voice. This was the medicine he needed.

"No. You're not disturbing me at all. Actually, I was just lying here…" *Feeling sorry for myself,* he thought.

"Oh, you must be tired. You've been traveling all week. I won't keep you. I can call another time."

"You're already on the phone, Dee. And I'm not that tired. How are you? You've been on my mind."

Her response sounded light, as if she was filled with joy. "I'm fine." She paused. "Why have I been on your mind?"

He grinned, encouraged by her new boldness. "For a number of reasons."

"Good ones, I hope."

"Absolutely."

"Well, in that case, I was wondering…if you're not busy…I mean, I know it's Friday and last minute, but I had a taste for ice cream."

The laughter started deep in his belly, rising and exploding in a burst that raced across the phone lines and seemed to tickle Deanna in the same place. She joined in.

Still giggling, she asked, "Is that a no?"

"How 'bout if I pick you up in an hour?"

"I'll be here."

After they devoured their favorite ice cream and Clay regaled Deanna with anecdotes about his trips and the eccentric characters that he'd met, he suggested that they take a ride.

"Where?"

"We could drive out to the South Street Seaport. There are tons of restaurants, shops along the boardwalk, and a jazz barge that is usually kicking on Friday night. How 'bout it?"

He watched an array of emotions dance across her face, mostly negative, he feared.

She pressed her lips together in a way he'd come to know that she was thinking.

"Could we stop home first so I can change?" Her smile was like a ray of sunshine bursting through the storm.

"Absolutely."

Deanna had changed into a sea-green pantsuit of some silky material that moved like gently lapping waves around her slender body. The wide-legged pants flowed with her every movement, giving her appearance of floating on air. The cinched jacket defined her narrow waist and accentuated her full, rounded breasts.

His whole body went on full alert when she walked into the room.

"You look incredible."

"Do I? I hope so." She smiled demurely. "Ready when you are."

"Your chariot awaits, princess." He tucked her arm through his and led her out to the car.

They spent the evening on the top deck of the floating barge—the starlit sky their canopy—with jazzy stylist Betty Carter crooning and scatting the night away.

"Would you like something else to drink, Dee?"

"No. Two glasses of wine are about my limit. Any more and you'll be carrying me home."

"That doesn't sound like such a bad idea," he whispered in her ear.

She lowered her head and bit back a smile. He could see the slight flush rise to her cheeks and wished that he could see her eyes. But for the first time since they met, she'd put on dark glasses when they got out of the car. He wondered why, but decided against asking. He was just happy that she'd gone out with him at all. Obviously she felt safe, somehow protected behind the dark lenses. As long as she was comfortable and out with him, that was what mattered. He wanted to tell her about Rachael, and most of all about Matthew. But tonight was their night. He'd have time.

They rode home quietly talking about the evening, Clay's impending trip, and Deanna's plans for launching the Institute, with soft music from the car stereo playing in the background.

Their idyll, however, was disrupted when the DJ announced the next sound selection would be from an old hit from legendary classical jazz pianist Deanna Winters.

He felt her stiffen, her words cut off in midsentence, as the music filtered through the speakers. The unmistakable artistry that was Deanna Winters enveloped them. The sultry, almost erotic riffs and downbeats rode with and through them. He could picture her behind the piano, eyes closed, head tossed back, wrapped in the magic of her music.

"That was from the Grammy Award winning CD *Turning Point* by Deanna Winters. Where is she now?" the deep voice of the DJ asked his faceless audience.

Clay turned to Deanna and took her hand, which was cold as ice.

"Are you all right?"

She nodded. "That was a surprise. I haven't heard my work on the air in a long time." Her voice was almost wistful, Clay thought.

"It's still the best."

"It takes me back. But...I can't go back."

"None of us can, Dee. Just forward."

"I've built this world of make-believe, Clay. And in it I'm just like everyone else. Or at least I can pretend to be. I've organized my home, my clothes, my habits, everything to conform to my secret garden. I don't interact with the rest of the world because...I've been afraid. Afraid to trip, walk into a wall, put on clothes that don't match. Afraid not to be able to maintain the standards everyone had come to expect from me. I've been afraid to cry for fear that I would encounter only pity.

"I've been afraid to care about anyone…again…for fear of being rejected because I'm blind. So, I've withdrawn into my fantasy. The world that I finally have control over. All my life my every action and thought were dictated by my parents, teachers, my riding instructors, tutors, maestros, record company executives, the listening audience." Her voice lowered. "And then you came along and cracked open the door to my secret garden. I want to take that step outside." She paused. "I want to stop being afraid."

"Where are you now, Deanna?"

She took off her glasses and faced him.

"At the turning point."

So am I, Clay thought.

"Do you want to come in for a little bit?" Deanna asked when they pulled up in front of her house.

"Sure. If you're not too tired."

"No. Actually I feel exhilarated. And there's something I'd like to talk with you about."

Deanna curled up on the love seat, tucking her feet beneath her. Apparently deep in thought, she twirled a lock of hair around her finger.

The silence was making Clay nervous. If she was going to tell him that she wanted to just keep things strictly business between them, he'd find a way to deal with it. It was the not knowing that was ticking like a time bomb in his stomach.

"So what did you want to talk with me about?"

She turned her head in the direction of his voice as if just realizing that he was still in the room.

"Oh. I'm sorry. I guess I was lost in my own thoughts." She smiled. "I've thought a lot about what you said about me playing. I've listened to Tracy badger me mercilessly about the same thing." She hesitated. "And hearing my music again finally put everything in perspective. The Institute, as you know, is being set up for music therapy. I'm going to teach again."

Clay sat up straighter. "That's fabulous, Deanna. You won't regret it, and I know your students couldn't ask for a better instructor. When are you doing to start?"

She grinned. "Probably sometime next week. I just need to let Tracy know so that she can get a schedule together for me."

"You haven't told her yet?"

"No. I was going to call her in the morning."

He'd been the first one. She thought that much of him to give him her news before anyone else. Even Tracy.

"You don't know how much this means to me."

"My playing again?"

"No. Well, that too. But that you shared your news with me."

"You were a big part of the decision."

"It had to start with you. Are you scared?"

"A little."

He rose and took her hand. "There's a great big old piano sitting right on the other side of this room, just begging you to come and play it. Why don't you?" he coaxed. "For me. For yourself. Sort of a semiprivate warm-up rehearsal."

He gave her hand a slight tug until she was on her feet, then led her to the piano. For several moments, she sat, hands clenched in her lap. Finally, she raised them, poised above the black and white keys.

A melody, soft, tantalizing, and haunting in its beauty, slowly, eloquently filled the room, filled the soul. Clay felt himself become one with the music, felt a lightness of spirit he hadn't experienced in far too long.

Her fingers glided, raced, pranced across the keys, and Clay was enchanted, mesmerized by the music and the transformation brought about in Deanna. She was euphoric. Her face glowed. The green of her eyes sparkled like emerald fire as she segued from one classic number to the next, until she came to a spiraling climax.

She sat, her head bent as if in prayer.

"That was magnificent," Clay whispered.

Deanna blinked as if coming back to herself. "Thank you."

He sat next to her on the bench. "The world still misses your playing. They have to."

"It was never the world I wanted to play for," she admitted. "I did it because…well, it gave me something to perform in front of thousands of people. It made me feel that I was cared about." She slowly shook her head. "But I know now that it's not really me, but my music."

"It is you, Dee. You are your music. It can't come alive like that under anyone else's fingertips. You put yourself into it. It stands to reason that your fans care as much about you as they do about your music. Your ability brings joy to millions." He stroked her face. "Now you can begin again by bringing that joy to the children."

She gave him a tight smile. "It's a start."

"We all have to start somewhere." He brushed her cheek with a kiss.

She nodded and slowly stood, moving away from the piano. "You're right." She made her way to the couch where Clay joined her.

"There's something I need to talk with you about too."

He told her about Rachael and Matt, about the divorce and the bitter results, Rachael's adultery—which he'd opted not to mention to the judge. "And now Rachael phoned to tell me she's moving back to New York. She wants me to spend more time with my son." He struggled to keep the pain out of his voice. "It'll be the first time that I get to see him in more than one year."

"You must miss him a lot." These were Deanna's first words since he began to speak. "I can't imagine what that must be like. To have a child and not be able to see him every day."

"There is no way to explain it. It's a pervasive emptiness that nothing can fill."

"Is that why you work so hard?"

It was as though she could see with her heart and straight into his soul.

"Yeah. Keeps my mind occupied."

"It will be good for your son to be with you, won't it?"

He released a heavy sigh, understanding that the question she posed wasn't what she really wanted to know. "I hope that it will be. It's hard to say. He may have forgotten all about me by now. I know it'll be difficult for me," he confessed.

"Why?"

"It's taken years, some counseling and a lot of soul-searching to get beyond what happened between me and Rachael. I'm at a point in my life when I'm starting to feel human again—want things, need things, people." His voice deepened. "A relationship in my life again. I'd been unwilling to take that chance before. I didn't think I'd be good for anyone in the mental state I was in. But that part of my life is behind me. Now here she comes to resurrect it all. I don't want any part of Rachael Holder-McDaniels-Graham. But to get to my son, I have to deal with her."

"Well, you were married once. You have a child together…"

"I don't want her back, Dee. I hope you believe that."

She didn't respond.

Gently he pulled Deanna into his arms, hearing all the things she didn't say, for the moment pushing away thoughts of everything other than her and his own needs. Deanna made him want to care again, to be the provider, the knight in shining armor. She made him want to be whole.

She relaxed against him, wrapping her arms around his waist, seeming to listen to the beat of his heart. Hesitantly she raised her head, lifting her face toward his. Her lids fluttered closed, shielding her eyes. Shaky fingers reached up and stroked his face.

Clay slid his hands through her hair, drawing her closer. He felt the warmth of her breath whisper across his mouth as he lowered his to meet her parted lips.

A deep sigh rushed from her lungs when their mouths fused, and the room seemed to shift as if a powerful undertow was pulling him out to sea.

He didn't want to scare her off again, no matter how good she was making him feel. She'd have to be the one to give him the green light to take the next step.

Reluctantly he eased back, his heart hammering in his chest. Tenderly he ran the tip of a finger along her cheek. "Only when you're ready, Dee," he whispered. "Not just vulnerable."

She pressed her lips together and turned away. "How will I know?"

He draped his arm around her shoulders. She shut her eyes.

"You'll know, Dee. Just like you knew when it was time to take that first walk with me, when it was time to play the piano again, when it was time to say yes to reentering the world. You'll know."

"When I'm with you I feel as if I could cross the line. But then something happens...and I get scared."

Clay took a breath. He knew he was taking a chance, but maybe if he could get her to talk about her fear of intimacy he could find a way to help her.

"Dee, what happened that has you so frightened? Will you talk to me about it?"

She shook her head. "I...it's just so ugly." She covered her face with her hands as if to hide some secret shame. "I don't want you to think less of me."

"How could I? Whatever happened couldn't have been your fault."

"It was my fault! I could have stopped him." Her voice rose. "I could have walked away. But I didn't."

"Why don't you try to start from the beginning?"

Clay ran his hand caressingly over her hair as she haltingly began to disclose her life with Cord, the sexual abuse and emotional control that had enveloped her life for three years; her naiveté in relationships, her pride that had sustained her, and her loyalty to a man who had some serious problems. But it was her strength that finally allowed her to walk away.

When she'd finished, exhausted and shaky, Clay was silent for several moments, searching for the words that would sooth her spirit and ease her sense of guilt.

"Every man isn't like Cord, Deanna." He stroked her face. "It may be hard for you to believe that, but it's true. Unfortunately, you wound up with the wrong man. It may sound easy for me to sit here and tell you to put it behind you. But I know it's not that easy. And it will take time." He paused gauging his next words. "Have you thought about counseling?"

She shook her had. "Not for this."

"Maybe you should. Maybe someone who's objective and who has had experience dealing with these things could help you work it out."

She tugged on her bottom lip with her teeth.

"Believe me, I've been there. I spent many an hour on a therapist's couch trying to get my life together after Rachael. I felt worthless, used, unworthy of being cared about. But I finally understood that what Rachael did had nothing to do with me as a person. That's just who she was."

"I don't think I can take any more counseling or therapy, Clay, voluntary or otherwise. Since my accident, counseling was required, part of the rehabilitation process. The past few years have been a nightmare of therapeutic sessions."

"It's your decision, and just a suggestion. We all have to find a way to deal with the things that bother us. You'll find your way too. Getting out in the world again, playing your music—even being with me—are all steps in that direction."

She released a long breath. "One day at a time?"

"Exactly." He leaned closer and touched his mouth to hers. "I'm here for you."

"You have your own life to worry about."

Her comment underscored his own thoughts. "Don't worry about me. Let's focus on you."

She smiled, and her dimple winked at him. "Have you ever been riding?"

CHAPTER X

Riding. Clay couldn't remember the last time he'd been riding. He'd probably make a complete fool of himself. Even if Deanna *couldn't* see, she'd been a championship rider. Probably still was. When she told him the night before that she wanted to ride her filly Dreammaker again, you could have knocked him over with a feather. It was the last thing he expected to hear, until she asked that he go with her. That really did it.

"It's something I have to do, for me, and I want you with me," she had said.

How could he resist? She was taking major leaps in her life. The least he could do was keep her from stumbling into the pitfalls—even if he couldn't keep himself from tumbling off a horse.

He kept a protective hand and a watchful eye on Deanna as they crossed the stable yard. But looking at her, she seemed as relaxed and comfortable as if she was walking around her own living room...as if she was letting the scent of hay, freshly cut grass, the sounds of pounding hooves, and the whinnying of horses to wrap around her like old friends.

Wistfully she said, "If I close my eyes I can almost see the main house and the stable hands grooming the horses, see them racing across the pasture, hurtling over the jumps and trotting in perfect step. I've missed this so much, Clay," she added with a hitch in her voice, as if the swell of buried sensations had rushed from the hidden place she'd stored them. "I didn't realize just how much until this moment."

Clay lightly squeezed her hand. "Then I'm glad you decided to do this, Dee. And that you want me to be a part of it." He kissed her cheek. "Wait here," he said, helping her to the bench that bordered the main house. "let me see if Dreammaker is ready."

He'd called earlier that morning and advised the owner, Howard Collins, that Deanna would be coming in from New York to ride but insisted on her privacy. Howard had assured him that it wouldn't be a problem and Dreammaker would be waiting. The man had been as good as his word.

Leading Dreammaker across the field to where Deanna sat, Clay could see the nervous energy pulse through her body. Her foot tapped out an uneven beat, while her hands threaded and unthreaded. When he walked up to her, she jumped.

"Here she is," he said gently. He reached down and took her hand, placing the reins in her grasp.

Slowly Deanna stood. Tears welled in her eyes as she reached out and stroked Dreammaker's silky mane. The horse whinnied her pleasure, nuzzling Deanna's face.

She pressed her cheek against Dreammaker's nose. "Hey, girl," she said, her voice wobbly. "I missed you."

Clay grinned, watching the exchange. "I think she missed you, too."

Deanna turned toward the sound of Clay's voice. "Clay...I...can't do this. I don't know what made me think I could."

"Of course you can. We'll do it together."

"Together?"

"I'll ride with you on Dreammaker. You didn't think I'd let you do this alone, did you?"

"Oh, Clay." Her face beamed with pleasure. "You are truly a gift."

He helped her into the saddle, mounted behind her with his arms around her waist as much for his safety as hers, and off they went.

Since he was pressed against her back, each rise and fall of their ride brought their bodies together in the most erotic of ways. Clay fought hard to concentrate on the ride and not the feel of his body wrapped protectively around hers. Urges that he'd kept at bay rushed from the depths of him, swirling like a rising storm.

Everything around him seemed to come alive, his own senses heightened to razor sharpness. He knew she could feel the rapid beat of his heart pump steadily against her back. Even her soft words of encouragement to him sent warming rays of desire racing through his bloodstream.

They rode for nearly an hour, and it seemed that neither wanted the exhilarating experience to end, until Deanna said she felt a storm coming.

"Thank you so much, Clay," Deanna said when they ran to the car, dodging the first drops of rain. "I never thought I'd ride again."

He clasped her folded hands with his right and drove with his left. "You can do anything you want, Dee. As long as you're willing to take a chance."

"Even drive?" she teased.

"W-e-l-l, I wouldn't go that far."

They laughed, and she wrapped her hand around his. She leaned her head back against the headrest and closed her eyes, a soft smile on her lips.

"I don't know how you rode so well, Clay," she murmured, stirring from a short nap.

"Hello sleepyhead."

She yawned. "I was just thinking or dreaming, that you seemed so comfortable on Dreammaker, and she with you. She's usually skittish around strangers. At least she used to be." Rain pummeled the windshield.

"Believe me, I wasn't as calm as I appeared," he said. *In more than one way.* He steered the car into the driveway.

"But you have a calming, gentle way that makes everyone and everything around you feel safe and secure," she murmured, as they ran hand-in-hand into the house. A brilliant bolt of lightning illuminated the gray sky.

She turned to him as he closed the door. Her face glowed as if lit with an inner light. Drops of rain glistened like diamonds on her ink-black hair. Her lips were slightly parted, waiting…He stared at her beautiful face, believing that she could almost see into his heart.

"Do *you* feel that way around me, Dee, safe and secure?"

"Yes."

His heart knocked against his chest. "I want to take care of you. Open the world to you through my eyes. I want to be the one you turn to."

He drew her closer and then his lips touched hers setting off tiny sparks of electricity between them.

Her breath caught as he subtly increased the pressure, his tongue cautiously stroking her lips until they parted, giving him access.

A soft moan floated upward, from deep within her as he drew her into his arms, shutting out the world.

Her fingers stroked and caressed his back as their bodies came together, line for line, curve for curve, hard and soft. Their mouths played teasing, taunting games with each other. Their hands began the slow art of exploration, awakening long suppressed desires.

But he wouldn't pressure her, he silently vowed, even as his need for her grew to breathless proportions.

"Dee," he groaned.

"Let's go upstairs," she whispered against his mouth, shaky fingers sliding from his back to take his hand.

His eyes searched for her face for any hint of doubt and found none.

He followed her up the carpeted stairway, down the hall, and into the bathroom where she turned on the shower full blast.

With her head lowered she began to unfasten the buttons of her shirt until Clay's hands stilled her fingers. "Let me."

The buttons came loose, one by one, almost in slow motion, Clay thought, until the shirt fell on the pink tiled floor, followed by the rest of her clothing, and then his.

His fingers caressed the curve of her breasts, causing the dark tips to peak and harden under his touch.

Deanna seemed to trace and chart a course along his body as if she was visualizing the smooth and, at some points, rough skin that covered his body, bringing his flesh alive with a heat that scorched him from the inside out.

"Dee," he moaned, locking his mouth to hers and drawing her into the pulsing spray of water.

Scented soap, streams of water, hands and mouths, slid over every inch of their bodies until they were weak from wanting.

Clay backed her up against the tiled wall, pressing his body against hers. He parted her thighs with a sideways brush of his leg and stood between them, the throb of his sex vibrating between her heat.

"I want you, Dee…so…much," he uttered in ragged whisper, rocking his hips against her.

She arched her neck as the water poured over them, the one element that kept the temperature from skyrocketing out of control.

"I'm not afraid. Not anymore. Just unsure of my…responses. Oh, Clay," she whimpered when he slid a finger along the sensitive bud and rubbed. Her legs began to tremble. "I don't know…If I will…can satis—"

"Sssh. Don't." He cupped her breasts, took one, then the other into his mouth. "Just let it happen." He turned off the water and scooped her up into his arms, covering her lips with his. "There's nothing to compare this with."

He carried her into the bedroom and laid her on the bed, momentarily standing over her, taking in the raw beauty before him. "We're going to create a new beginning."

Cautiously he eased down beside her, cradling her body, whispering soft words of assurance while his hands stroked her, slowly allaying the last of her doubts.

"Slow and easy, Dee. I wanna take my time with you." He increased the pressure of his touch.

"Yes," she breathed. "Now, Clay…now."

He kissed her then, the way he'd dreamed, with all the need, all the longing that he'd held inside. With a patience that belied his rising need, he placed his body atop hers, bracing his weight on his arms. He dipped his head and suckled one ripe nipple, then the other, her soft erotic whimpers inflaming him until he thought he'd burst. But he waited, he took his time, playing with and taunting her body until there was no denying her readiness to accept him. And still he played with her. His mouth tasting and exploring her sweet, wet flesh—lower, inch by inch until he reached her center and tenderly separated the moist folds to expose the throbbing bud. And he tasted of her, like a child enraptured by the sweetness of ice cream, licking over and over until he felt her body tense, her fingernails claw his back, her hips arch, her body shudder with the force of her climax—until tears coursed down her cheeks.

Slowly he made his way back up her body, placing tiny kisses along her belly, upward, to capture a honeyed nipple between his teeth.

Emotions, sensations, and raw need raged unchecked. Never before had he felt so hot, so needy for the feel of being sucked into a woman's body. When he felt his thick stiffness probe her, separate and enter her body, starbursts erupted from his sex where she held him and jettisoned upward to explode in his head like a million twinkling lights.

"Oh, God," he groaned, only by sheer will containing his climax, when he felt her deep tunnel begin to contract and suck him in.

"I want you, Clay. All of you," she moaned. "Please." She rocked her hips against him, and he cried out in pleasure.

"That's how I'm going to give myself to you," he rumbled in her ear, capturing her legs and draping them over his shoulders. "Just as you're going to give yourself to me." Descending into her depths, he covered her mouth with his, sealing off her cry. The air that swished out of her lungs as he rose and fell within her, rushed into his, and it was as if their souls united.

Slow, fast, deep, short, rocking, rotating, mouths, hands, they were everywhere—together, one unit, blending, discovering—giving until they could give no more, the pressure too great, the need for release too urgent to contain, and they exploded, one setting off the other in a cacophony of unintelligible words and shuddering bodies that had reached the apex of satisfaction.

Clay stroked her hair, traced a path down her cheek, then placed a tender kiss there. "How are you?"

"Never better. I...don't believe it could be this way."

"It, this can be even better." He caressed her spine. "Give me half a chance and I'll prove it to you again and again."

"Is that a threat or a promise, Mr. McDaniels?"

"It's a vow, Deanna Winters. From the bottom of my heart, it's a vow."

The rain slapped naughtily against the windowpane, begging entry even as the thunder rolled over the horizon. But all they heard was the beat of their hearts.

CHAPTER XI

Clay paced the expanse of his living room floor, into the kitchen, downstairs to the den, back up to the master bedroom. He'd checked the clocks so often, the swinging second hand was making him dizzy.

He'd spent the early part of the morning running to the store for all kinds of snacks, cleaning the house, and talking to Deanna about their incredible night together and his apprehension about his day. He'd wanted to spend the night, the day, the rest of his life, with her lying in his arms. It had been Deanna who had sent him packing so that he could be ready when his son arrived.

That made him smile. She was...words escaped him.

He checked the clock again. Where was Rachael? She was deliberately making him sweat. Maybe she wasn't going to show up at all. Maybe this whole thing was one big joke. Maybe...

The doorbell rang. His body jerked as if he'd been shot with stun gun effectiveness. He took a deep breath and went down the stairs to the front door.

They faced each other for the first time in ages. She was still heart-stoppingly beautiful. Her rich, brown color was heightened by the summer sun. The perfect heart-shaped face that had once haunted his dreams was surrounded by a cap of close-cropped curls. The full lips that had committed wickedly sinful acts on his body were still the same. Ready. But it was always her doe-shaped eyes, the color of bee-spun honey, that unceasingly had the power to mesmerize him, stir him deep in his loins. He fought down the sensation.

"Hello, Rachael."

She smiled, and those damned eyes sparkled like fine wine. "Hello, Clay." She stepped aside to give him the first view of his son in more than a year.

He bent down, his eyes roving over Matthew, his heart knocking in his chest. "Hello, son," he whispered, afraid that if he even spoke too loud, this miracle would cease to exist.

Matthew looked at his father for a long moment, then a tentative smile inched across his face. He grabbed his mother's hand. "Hi," he squeaked.

He was so beautiful, Clay thought, so perfect. How much he'd missed him, missed what they could have been sharing together. He swallowed down the knot in his throat. "Hi, baby." He stroked his son's cheek, and bit down on his lip from keep it from trembling when Matthew suddenly rushed into his arms, burying his face in his chest.

The tightness constricted in his chest as he hugged the tiny version of himself snugly against him, inhaling the soap-and-water scent. Slowly he stood, lifting Matthew in his arms.

"Daddy missed you, Matt. A whole lot."

"I talk to him about you all the time. He has all the cards...and the toys," Rachael said softly.

Clay gazed at her and, remarkably, saw the truth in her eyes. "Thank you."

She nodded. "I thought you two might want to get reacquainted. So I'll leave you two alone."

His ears must be playing tricks on him. "Excuse me?"

She bent down and picked up a *Sesame Street* knapsack that was resting at her feet and handed it to him. "Everything you might need is in there," she said, with what appeared to be a sad smile on her face.

She rose on tiptoe and kissed Matthew's cheek, then gave him a tight squeeze. "Be a good boy, sweetie."

"Okay."

She gave Clay a tight smile, turned and went down the stairs.

Somebody pinch me, Clay thought. *This can't be real.*

"Well, buddy, what do you like to do?"

"Play Nintendo, and play with my Superman. You wanna hear me count to one hundred?"

Clay tossed his head back and laughed with pure delight. "I sure do."

The hours raced by. They had a supersized meal at McDonalds, played catch in Central Park, took a trip to the famed FAO Schwartz toy store and bought a brand-new Nintendo system along with six game cartridges. And Matthew beat his dad mercilessly at every game. His son was a techno whiz, Clay thought with pride. Matthew told him stories about his friends in New Jersey, his favorite teacher in his kindergarten class, and his trip to the zoo.

By five o'clock they were both exhausted and hungry. Anticipating that Rachael would be returning soon, Clay decided to order a pizza to hold them over until she arrived.

He could get used to this, he thought, watching his son pick the cheese off his pizza and slurp it into his mouth. But what kind of life could he offer a child when he spent so much time away from home? If Rachael was serious, he'd have to consider cutting back on his globe hopping. And what about Deanna? How would she fit into the picture?

"Finished!" Matthew announced.

"Let's get those hands and face washed and I'll challenge you in another game of Nintendo."

Matthew whooped with joy and darted out of the kitchen to the half-bath down the hall.

When Clay checked the time next, they were well into a third game. It was after eight. Where was Rachael? A sensation of foreboding settled in his stomach. The few times she had allowed him to visit with Matthew, she appeared like clockwork at the appointed time, as if making certain that he wouldn't gain one extra minute. Something was wrong. Now that he thought about it, she'd never said what time she'd be back. That wasn't like her.

"I'm sleepy, Daddy," Matthew mumbled, putting the controller for the game on the floor. He laid his head down on Clay's lap and stuck his thumb in his mouth.

"Mommy should be here any minute, buddy. Don't fall asleep."

"Mommy's not coming," Matt mumbled over his thumb.

"Of course she is. She's just late."

"She said I could stay here with you." Matt's eyes closed.

Clay's heart raced. He couldn't have heard right, and Matt had to be mistaken. He looked down at this son, his thoughts scurrying in a million different directions at once.

Not coming.

Gently he eased away and stood, then began pacing the floor. He had no idea where or how to reach her. He hadn't bothered to ask her where they were staying. He hadn't seen the need. Now he wished he had. What in the hell was going on?

He looked over at his sleeping son. Well, he couldn't just leave him on the floor. He'd put him to bed for the time being, Rachael was bound to show up.

But what if she didn't?

After getting Matthew settled in bed, Clay retreated to the living room and absentmindedly began to pick up the remnants of their day. He took Matthew's knapsack with the intention of putting it in the bedroom, but something made him open it.

It was filled with action figures, several changes of clothes, and a toothbrush. He started to close it when he spotted a small white envelope.

He pulled it out and read the unbelievable contents, and his whole life changed in a matter of moments.

The thundering sound of applause from the limo's television set or, rather, from the crowd at Radio City Music Hall, roused Clay from his reminiscing. The musical tribute had just completed, and the onstage movie screen was again filled with Deanna's face.

The emcee returned to the podium and introduced the next guest, via satellite, the President of the United States.

Tonight was definitely her night. Clay smiled, mulling over the turn of events that had joined his and Deanna's lives over the past two years. But where would they be in this time tomorrow? He worried. It was he who had inadvertently led her to what could be her salvation from darkness. *Dr. Marcus Chandler.*

But when Deanna stepped back into the light, would she still need and want him? She had helped him to become all he could be, a true father and a friend. Through her, he'd learned the art of trust. He was able to love again. And he was selfishly afraid that before the evening was over, the world that he knew would change…and Deanna with it. How would she react when she finally saw him?

The limo pulled to a stop in front of Radio City. Clay dashed intside.

CHAPTER XII

Seated midway in the orchestra section, Marcus Chandler watched the showcase of events with a mixture of awe and apprehension. Deanna had asked him to come tonight, and he hoped that she had finally reached a decision. But she hadn't alluded to that in her letter requesting his attendance.

In the months that he'd grown to personally know Deanna, he'd realized that she was her own woman who would do things her own way. Perhaps, initially, her blindness derailed her road to greatness, but through pure determination of will she'd surpassed even her own high standards. She had rebuilt her life and everything in it. She'd taken a handicap that would have sent many to the gallows of despair, and turned it into her own crusade. A crusade for those who couldn't fight for themselves.

Still, he believed she could be even more than she was, and he had the power in his skilled hands to give her back what many would rather die for than lose.

Yet she'd hesitated. True, the operation had never been performed on a human subject, but his skill and his research had proven, at least to him, that she would be the one who could take his career to unimaginable heights.

But was he himself blinded to the truth? Were his deep feelings for Deanna keeping him from seeing the dangers involved? Did he want to win her heart and the acclaim of worldwide recognition so desperately that he was willing to risk everything in the hope of restoring her vision? Was her gratitude an equal substitute for the love he craved from her? He knew, for her, it would never be. But he could make her love him. If only she'd let him. But the Atlantic Ocean and thousands of miles and philosophical differences remained between them.

He sighed heavily and leaned farther back into the red plushness of his seat. *Deanna*. From the moment Clay McDaniels had introduced him to her at a benefit at the White House, Marcus knew he could change her life.

Just as she'd changed his...

The reception hall of the White House sparkled with political dignitaries, actors, musicians, business powerhouses, doctors, lawyers, and Indian chiefs in attendance at the thousand-dollar-per-plate re-election dinner.

The last time Marcus had seen Clay McDaniels they were both dining in an outdoor café in Paris. Clay was alone—a state that Marcus often found him in when they ran into each other—totally absorbed in a stack of papers in front of him. Seeing Clay tonight was not what surprised him. The dynamic and quietly powerful McDaniels was sure to be at any major event where large sums of money and power were involved. Some of the who's who milling about the White House were some of McDaniels's best clients. What did surprise him was that Clay was accompanied by Deanna Winters. He'd heard rumors. But he never paid attention to rumors. He'd heard enough about himself to write a book. According to the tabloids, his reputation as an international playboy was almost as unmatched as his surgical skills.

Since the accident, Deanna Winters had pretty much lived the life of a recluse until she'd launched the Deanna Winters Foundation and then the Institute, which had gained international recognition under her guidance, and this devout admiration. But her whereabouts and her progress were not unknown to him.

Her tragic loss of sight had become a catalyst, giving him the desire to complete the controversial research he'd put aside. He began to dedicate all of his free time to perfecting the technique that would restore Deanna Winters's vision. To do what would be his greatest triumph.

On numerous occasions he'd tried to contact her but had been unsuccessful. Still, he pursued his dream. Completion of his research was months away, but he knew he was close. He could feel it in the tingle of his fingertips.

He'd always admired her, but only as an entertainer and equestrienne. Since he'd devoted the last two years of his life to finding the cure for her, he'd read everything ever written about her, listened to every recording she'd ever made, viewed videotapes of her riding championships. He was mesmerized by her, intrigued, and totally captivated. To him, she had become more of an icon *after* the accident than before. But just imagine what she could do with her sight restored. The possibilities were limitless. He would make it happen.

Marcus excused himself from his dining companion, a statuesque Ethiopian model who made it a point to see him whenever she was in the country, and made his way over to where Clay was seated.

"Clay, good to see you again."

Clay twisted in his seat to face him. "Marcus, I didn't know you'd be here tonight. Had you pegged for a Republican," he joked, taking Marcus's outstretched hand. "How are you and the wonderful world of medicine?"

Marcus chuckled. "Busy as ever on both counts."

"Deanna, let me introduce Dr. Marcus Chandler. Marcus, Deanna Winters."

Deanna turned in the direction of Marcus's voice as he greeted her and tilted her head upward. The slow, easy smile that slid across her exquisite sandy-colored face was like watching the sun languidly rise across the horizon, casting its warming rays over all in its path.

The emerald orbs, though slightly dulled, as if they needed polishing, still held signs of life. And he would have sworn that she could see him. That, he knew, took the utmost skill and determination, relentless training, and razor-sharp sensitivity to the environment. It took a special kind of person to master the technique. Most failed.

He suddenly felt hot inside, in awe and at a total loss. Here before him was the woman to whom he'd dedicated many a waking hour, and he couldn't find the right words to say.

"Pleasure to meet you, Dr. Chandler. English," she added with a smile, noting his barely-there British accent.

Her voice was like a rough whisper, sultry and inviting. Did she work at that, too, or was it as natural as her beauty?

She extended a hand, which Marcus took and brought to his lips.

"Believe me, Ms. Winters, the pleasure is mine. And yes, you're correct. London. You have a good ear."

"What type of medicine do you practice, Mr. Chandler?"

"I'm an ophthalmic surgeon. I specialize in sight restoration techniques." He saw the flush infuse her cheeks, and she blinked rapidly before smiling tightly. "A very challenging profession, I'm sure."

Clay threw a scathing look in Marcus's direction, which he ignored.

"It can be very rewarding, Ms. Winters, but it has its setbacks, too. I'd like to speak with you about it sometime. I've been studying your case."

"Perhaps...you can call me in New York. If you can contact the Foundation, they know how to reach me."

"I'll do that. I'm sure you'll be pleased with what I have to tell you. Enjoy your evening." His gaze reached Clay and captured a look he couldn't pinpoint—almost one of jealousy.

Returning to his table, he glanced in their direction and saw them with their heads bowed together in what appeared to be an intense conversation. He wondered if it was about him.

He turned his attention back to his dining companion, his thoughts were consumed with Deanna Winters. He'd finally met her, and she was willing to speak with him again. Soon he would he able to prove his greatness to the world—and to her.

He didn't want to seem too eager, so after returning to his home in London, he waited several days before attempting to contact her. When he did, remarkably, he was put right through, and she actually sounded happy to hear from him, almost anxious.

"Dr. Chandler, I'm so glad you called. I thought you'd forgotten me."

"That would be absolutely impossible, Ms. Winters."

"Deanna."

"If you call me Marcus."

"Deal." She laughed, and it sounded like music. "Now what are we these wonderful things you want to tell me?"

They talked for nearly an hour with Marcus explaining how he'd designed a microscopic computer chip that, when connected behind the eye, had the ability to restore sight, but only in those whose sight had been lost through damage, nothing congenital.

"It sounds as if you've uncovered a modern-day miracle, Marcus. I'd like you to send as much information as possible to the Foundation. I'll have my staff review it, and if everything is in order, we'd be thrilled to send a major contribution to continue the funding of your research."

For several seconds he sat in stunned silence. This was not what he expected at all.

He cleared his throat. "That's…very generous of you, but I designed the chip with you in mind."

A long train of silence hung between them.

Finally, Deanna spoke. "I…can't begin to express my gratitude. The amount of time, energy, and research involved is incomprehensible to me. I'm sure that you'll find the answer, but I'm not the one to try your technique on, Marcus. There are so many others out there who need and want their sight more desperately than I will ever need mine. Take the money that the Foundation will give you and use it. We have hundreds of children who come to the Institute for musical therapy. There has to be one among them that would be a perfect candidate. We'd even be willing to pay the medical expenses if everything pans out."

"Maybe if I came to New York, talked with you in person."

"I'm sure it won't change my mind, but please do come. I'd love for you to visit the Institute and meet the children."

"I'll do that under one condition."

"What's that?"

"When I come to New York, you promise to have dinner with me during my stay and listen to my proposition."

She laughed her musical laugh. "Sounds like blackmail."

"Is that a yes?"

"That's a possibility. Call me when you get to New York. We'll see what happens." She gave him her direct number and hung up.

Marcus released the breath he'd been holding. At least she sort of agreed to meet with him. Once he could talk to her in person, take her to dinner, tell her about the wonderful progress he'd made, he was sure he'd get her to agree. Who wouldn't jump at the opportunity to regain her sight?

He looked at the phone and heard Deanna's voice telling him that others needed their sight more than she'd ever need hers. What kind of woman was she? Really?

CHAPTER XIII

For the next few weeks Marcus worked tirelessly, day and night, collecting data, running tests. He served as the keynote speaker at the American Medical Association's symposium in Paris, where he gained substantial support for his research from the medical community.

During his spare moments, which were few and far between, he called Deanna to keep her abreast of his progress. Those rare moments were well worth the grueling hours he spent on his research.

"I heard about your presentation in Paris. Congratulations, Marcus."

He could almost see her radiant smile, and the sincere enthusiasm was unmistakable in her voice. "Believe me, I wish I could take all the credit. I have a dedicated research team who does a damned good job making me look good. There's no way I'd be where I am without them."

"I know how you feel. My staff, both at the Foundation and the Institute, are the ones who make things happen. All I can do is lend my name whenever it will help our cause."

"You're much more than just a name, Deanna. You used your own tragedy to help others. Not many people can say that. That's what makes people more than just a name, or just an agency to funnel money through. And then again, you're lucky that you do have a name and a reputation behind you. You aren't as prone to run up against bureaucracy, set up for no other purpose than to get in your way."

She laughed softly. "You sound as though you've experienced it firsthand."

"Trust me, I have. Research grants are what the great debates thrive on. The competition is fierce and cutthroat, and the funding sources want to hold on to as much of their money for as long as possible."

"Sometimes I wonder where my life and my interests would be directed if I hadn't lost my sight. What would be important to me now?"

Marcus was quiet, contemplating her words, letting the question linger between them.

"Well," she said, "no sense in wallowing in what ifs. My course has been set, and so has yours."

"Speaking of courses, I'll be coming to New York next week. I hope you haven't forgotten your *almost* promise to have dinner with me."

She laughed. "I haven't forgotten. When will you be coming in?"

"I have an early morning flight scheduled for Wednesday."

"Great. Why don't we plan something for Friday evening?"

"Where would you like to go?"

"Right here."

His brows creased. "Here?"

"I'll fix dinner. At my house."

"You don't have to go to any special trouble."

"No trouble at all. As a matter of fact, maybe I'll have a small dinner party. I'll invite Clay and my assistant, Tracy. I know she's anxious to meet you."

His spirits sunk. His hopes for seeing her alone, temporarily halted. "If you're sure."

"Absolutely. Give me a call when you get in town. Where will you be staying?"

"At the Plaza."

"You have excellent taste. The Plaza has the best service. When I traveled into New York City and didn't want to go home, I stayed there."

Her voice sounded wistful, he thought. "Maybe you'll get a chance to visit me there while I'm in town. See if the service is still up to par."

"I don't want to make any promises. Now that I'm teaching again, my days are pretty tied up."

"Let's just play it by ear. I'll be in New York for at least a month."

"Can you stay away from your research that long?"

"Things are moving along extremely well. I'm sure my team can run things successfully in my absence. Besides, I want to spend some of my time convincing you that my procedure will work. Among other things," he added pointedly.

She cleared her throat. "Give me a call when you arrive," she said, sidestepping his not too subtle come-on.

"I will. I'm looking forward to seeing you again."

Slowly he hung up the phone, second-guessing himself. He shouldn't have tried to push her on the issue. It was obvious from her change in tone that she'd backed away. Yet he desperately wanted to ask her about the extent of her and Clay's relationship. How serious was it? Or was it strictly business?

CHAPTER XIV

Marcus squeezed his rented burgundy El Dorado into an available space halfway down the block from Deanna's house. He had mixed feelings about the evening. Although he was anxious to see her again, he wasn't eager to share the evening with others. He was sure if he could get her alone, spend some time with her, he could convince her to take the risk.

He wanted to submit his article to the *New England Journal of Medicine*, and he wanted to include that his procedure would be used on Deanna Winters. He had less than two months. But in that time, he felt certain, he would change her mind.

He walked up the short flight of steps to Deanna's two-story brownstone and rang the bell. Moments later it was answered by a stunning woman dressed in a form-fitting jersey knit dress in a flattering lavender.

"Hi, you must be Dr. Chandler," she said, extending a professionally manicured hand. There was an awesomeness in her wide-set brown eyes that clearly stated, "don't take me for granted," and yet she had an open look about her oval face that invited you to be friendly. "I'm Tracy Moore. Deanna has told me wonderful things about you and your work. I've been looking forward to finally meeting you. Please, come in."

She led the way, with him getting an eyeful of her well-defined posture. "Dee and Clay are in the living room." She cast him a look over her shoulder. "Deanna has put on a real spread. I know you'll like it."

Clay rose when Tracy and Marcus stepped into the archway of the living room. His smile was warm, but it didn't seem to reach his eyes, Marcus noted as he crossed the room, extending his hand.

"Good to see you again, Clay. Looking well."

"I have to work hard at it." Clay clapped him on the back. "How was your flight?"

"A bit bumpy," he said, his light British accent creeping through. "But it's to be expected." He turned his attention to Deanna, who'd angled her head in the direction of his voice. He bent down and took her hand, bringing it to his lips. "Still as beautiful as I remembered." She wore her shoulder-length black hair pulled on top of her head, so that it fell in a cascade of natural ringlets around her crown. Her smooth sandstone complexion was devoid of makeup save for a natural warm blush of her cheeks and the creamy bronze she'd stroked across her full mouth. The soft, clingy floor-length dress in a pale green reflected her eyes which seemed to zero right in on him.

"Flattery will get you a full-course meal tonight," she teased. "Please, make yourself comfortable. The bar is stocked, and I hope the hors d'oeuvres will hold you over until dinner. We're going to eat in about a half hour."

"Sounds fine."

"Can I fix you a drink?" Clay walked to the bar, tossing the question over his shoulder.

"Gin and tonic if you have it." *Playing host? How cozy.*

"So, Dr. Chandler," Tracy began, crossing her legs. "I understand you've done some remarkable work over the past few years. I read the reports you sent and was truly impressed."

He smiled, running his forefinger along the slim line of his mustache. "I enjoy what I do. When I went into medicine, it was to be able to make significant changes, in the medical profession and for the people who come to me for treatment."

Clay handed him a glass. "What kind of problems have you encountered with this *new* procedure of yours, Marcus?"

Marcus gave him a sharp look, perceiving Clay's tone as condescending, almost confrontational. *So that's how it's going to be.* He cleared his throat. "The most difficult problem to overcome is the same as in any implant procedure: rejection and infection."

Clay nodded, and Tracy took a quick look at Deanna, whose faced remained unreadable.

"But there are other concerns," Tracy cut in. "I noticed in your reports that there is no guarantee that that the procedure, once perfected, will last. Isn't that right?"

A warm flush invaded his body. "As I said, we still have a few months of testing before I'll be certain that the procedure is perfected."

He could feel skeptical eyes boring into him, feel their doubt. He had to convince them of the worth of this procedure. They had Deanna's ear.

The sudden lull in conversation was diffused only by the soft wounds of Wynton Marsalis and his trumpet coming through the built-in speakers.

"I think it's about time we all sat down to dinner," Deanna announced, effectively cutting through the tension. "Marcus is my guest, and you're both grilling him as if he sat in the witness stand. I'm sure there'll be plenty of opportunity to talk business at a later time. After I slaved over a hot stove all day, I know I don't want my digestion interrupted with shop talk. Now, come on into the dining room," she ordered.

Instinctively Marcus made a move to take Deanna's arm, which seemed to prompt the same response in Clay. They stood in awkward tableau, neither willing to back down.

Seeming to feel their dilemma, Deanna turned her head from one to the other, a devilish smile framing her bronze-covered lips. "Now if I can't find my way into my own dining room, I'm going to send myself back to rehab classes. Go, go," she shooed. "Before all the good seats are taken."

Marcus and Clay cast sheepish looks at each other, then headed for the dining room.

Dinner was friendly, full of lively conversation and travel anecdotes, the battle lines of protectiveness that both Clay and Tracy had drawn around Deanna temporarily forgotten.

Listening to Deanna direct and engage in the flow of conversation from politics to religion and everything in between, Marcus became more enamored of her. She was, for lack of a better word, extraordinary. She was totally secure within herself, not threatened at all by her blindness, but rather challenged by it.

"Clay turned me into a fiend for ice cream ages ago," Deanna said, flashing what appeared to be an intimate smile in Clay's direction. "So, guess what's for dessert."

"I'll get it," Tracy offered, excusing herself from the table.

"Let me help you." Marcus set his linen napkin on the table and followed Tracy into the kitchen.

"The bowls are in the cabinet above the microwave," Tracy said, turning toward the deep freezer to remove a gallon of French vanilla ice cream.

"How long have you known Deanna?" Marcus put the bowls on the Formica counter as Tracy began spooning out large dollops of smooth confection.

"We met in college. I was taking a finance course and Deanna took the class just to fill her schedule. She didn't have a clue what the professor was talking about and asked me if I could help her decipher her notes." She laughed, remembering. "We hit it off and have been friends ever since."

"So you knew her before the accident?"

Her eyes locked with his as if she were trying to see beyond the surface to the underlying reason for his question.

"Yes. I did." She spooned ice cream into the last bowl. "Why?"

Tracy looked him over for a long moment. "That was then. This is who she is now." She turned away, returning the tub of ice cream to the freezer. "There's a serving tray on top of the refrigerator. Would you mind?"

He pulled down the tray and handed it to her. However, he didn't let go. "I didn't mean to offend you, or ask anything that's too painful to answer. It's just that she's so incredible as she is now, I only wondered…"

"Everyone who comes in contact with her now wants to know the same thing. The bottom line, Marcus, is Deanna made a transition from where and who she was to where and who she is. I wouldn't presume to compartmentalize the then and the now. All I know is, she's my friend, my business partner, my sister. And I'll always do whatever is in my power to see that she's safe. I make sure that people don't take advantage of her generosity, her goodness, her willingness to help others, even at the expense of her own welfare. That's what I do, Marcus. That's all I do. And I'm damned good at it."

She pinned him a look, and though she was smiling, he could see the hard edge beneath the soft, feminine exterior. She might have been talking generalities, but she left no doubt that her declaration was directed at him. For a moment, his stomach muscles clenched.

"This stuff is going to melt if we don't get it in there soon," Tracy said, and his unease was gone as quickly as it had come.

"I thought you two had skipped town," Deanna quipped when they reappeared in the dining room.

"Just getting to know each other a bit better," Tracy said, taking her seat.

Clay cut Marcus a look but said nothing.

"Dinner was wonderful," Marcus said, slipping into his lightweight black Burberry trenchcoat.

"I'm glad you enjoyed it." Deanna stood in the open doorway. "I think you made quite an impression on Clay and Tracy."

"What makes you say that?"

"They've both designated themselves as my guardian angels. They devote all their free time to making sure that my life runs smoothly and that I don't make any rash decision." She smiled. "The truth is, I only allow them to think that I don't know what they're up to because it makes life a lot easier, and I love them both for it. So I hope you weren't offended that they put you under the interrogation lights. They seem to relish working the 'good cop, bad cop' routine."

Marcus laughed. "It was difficult for me to tell who was who at times."

"They've been doing the routine together for so long now, they begin to pick up each other's cross-examination habits."

"I'll try to remember that." He leaned down and placed a soft kiss at her temple. "I had a wonderful evening. You're an incomparable host. I hope you'll invite me back before I return to London."

She took an almost imperceptible step back. Her smile was fixed, her voice tremulous. "I will. Thank you for coming. Tracy will be in touch with you about a tour of the Institute."

"I'll be looking forward to it," he said, fighting to keep the sarcasm out of his voice. "Good night, Deanna."

"Good night, Marcus. Drive safely."

He turned and hurried down the steps. The door closed before he could reach the bottom.

CHAPTER XV

The Institute, which was actually an annex of the Deanna Winters Foundation, was a rehabbed four-story brownstone on the Upper West Side of Manhattan and tucked unobtrusively between a row of similar buildings.

Marcus walked up the steps to the parlor floor and rang the bell. Moments later, a young woman who couldn't have been more than eighteen answered the door, a warm smile of greeting on her face. Music and the sound of childish voices floated around her from the interior of the stately building.

"May I help you?"

"I'm Dr. Chandler. I have an appointment to see Tracy Moore."

"Come in. Ms. Moore is waiting for you in her office." She stepped aside to let him pass, then led him down a short hall to an office in the back. She knocked on the closed door.

"Come in," he heard Tracy call from beyond the polished mahogany door. She rose when Marcus entered. "Good to see you again, Marcus. We have several classes in session that I'm sure you'll enjoy. You can hang your coat on that hook." She pointed to a brass hook screwed into the wall. "And you can leave your briefcase by the desk."

Tracy led him to the top floor, where three rooms were set up for musical instruction. In one of the rooms, six children of varying ages sat around a piano with Deanna.

"This is Deanna's favorite room," Tracy said in a hushed whisper as they peeked inside, mindful of not disturbing the in-session practice. "This is one of the advanced classes. Most of these children have been with us since the Institute opened a year ago. This class should run for about another twenty minutes. Deanna will join us then." She quietly shut the door. "In the meantime, let me show you the rest of the facility."

They moved in and out of the various rooms on the top floor, then made their way down.

"We have a child psychiatrist on staff who evaluates each child upon admission, a nutritionist, a physical therapist, and teachers trained to work with handicapped children," Tracy informed him as they walked. "Most of the students have been blind since birth, or have been declared legally blind. There are a few who lost their sight through a genetic degeneration, others by tragic accidents. Based on some of the techniques I read in your reports, there are quite a few of our children who could benefit from your services," she concluded as they returned to her office.

"Would you care for lunch? I think baked chicken is on the menu for today."

"No, I'm fine, thanks. Are the children here all day?"

"Some of them. We offer regular school classes for grades K through five. Deanna was determined when she opened the Institute to provide the full gamut of services. We hope to expand the school portion of the program to the eighth grade."

"This is an extraordinary facility. I've never seen anything like it. It should be a model for replication."

"Perhaps it's something I'll consider," Deanna said, easing into the room.

Marcus turned in his seat, then stood, taking her in with one swift look. She was casually dressed in a pale peach jogging outfit. With her hair pulled back in a ponytail and bright white sneakers on her feet, she looked like a student herself.

"You definitely should. I've traveled around the world and I've never seen a setup that is so comprehensive. You've done something that no one has thought to do."

Deanna closed the door behind her. "Once I'm certain that we're on solid ground, I just might. But in the meantime, closing of the Institute will have to wait." She felt her way to a chair and sat down.

"Well, if you two will excuse me," Tracy said. "I have an appointment." She opened a desk drawer and pulled out her purse, draping the leather strap over her shoulder. "Dee, I'll talk with you tomorrow." She stuck out her hand toward Marcus. "Good to see you again, doctor."

"You, too." He shook her hand, opened the door for her, then turned back to Deanna.

"So you've had the grand tour." Deanna smiled. "What else is on your agenda for the day?"

"I was hoping to spend the day with you. If you're not busy," he quickly added.

"I have one more class." She flipped open the crystal on her watch and felt for the placement of the hands. "In about a half an hour." She snapped the crystal closed. "I'll be free after that."

"I spotted a nice restaurant not too far from here. I thought we might have an early supper."

She turned her gaze away "I...don't know if that's such a good idea."

He frowned. "Any reason?"

"I'd rather go home," she said, her voice low but definite.

"Whatever you want."

She looked as if she were relieved, and he wondered why.

She rose. "Feel free to wait here if you like. Or you can walk around."

"Would it be a problem if I sat in on your class?"

"No. I'd like that." She smiled, her momentary discomfort seeming to ease.

Marcus watched her, wondering what it was she was so afraid of. It was apparent that she was leery of something. Did she not want to be seen with him? But that was ridiculous. Or was it something else?

"My class is upstairs," she said, interrupting his twisting thoughts. "I want to get set up."

Marcus followed Deanna and sat at the far end of the spacious music room. The cathedral ceiling and high, arching windows blended seamlessly together to produce the perfect creative atmosphere. The last afternoon sun streamed through the crystal-clear windows and cast a warm, golden glow over the gleaming wood floor and the attentive faces of Deanna's students.

Watching her with her students, Marcus was able to witness yet another facet of the eclectic Deanna Winters. She was totally at ease, completely in her element. She had a natural, gentle manner and treated the six boys and girls as if they were the most important people in the world.

It was apparent they all adored her and hung on her every word, each one basking in her praise and attention.

When the session was over and the students left, Deanna collected the Braille music books and began stacking them in the built-in wall cabinets. She moved around the sunlit room with an easy, practiced grace. No movement was wasted. She was in total control of her space, and her precision fascinated him. There was no fumbling, no disorientation. To the unaware observer, Deanna presented herself as a sighted person. And that was when it hit him. This was the reason why she didn't want to go out with him. She would have no control over her space. For her it would be like walking out of the light she'd created around herself, into a pitch-black abyss.

His heart softened even more toward her. For all of her strengths, a fear of mishap was her Achilles' heel. But if she would only give him the chance, he could manage that. He was sure of it, and more determined than ever to make her realize it as well.

"All done," she announced. "My car should be out front. Did you drive?"

"Yes. I'll just follow you and meet you at your house. Or I could drive us both."

He watched her hesitate and thought she'd say no.

She pulled the phone toward her and pressed three buttons. "Paul, it's Dee. I won't need you tonight. A friend has offered to drive me home." She started to laugh. "Yes, Paul, I'm sure I'll be safe. No. You don't have to follow. Yes, I'll call when I get in." She laughed again. "I promise. Now go home and say hello to Gwynne for me."

She returned the receiver to the cradle, a soft smile lifting her mouth. "My driver, Paul, whom I 'inherited' from a friend, doesn't trust me in the car of any other driver. He's very protective."

"It seems that everyone in your life wants to protect you."

"Yes," she said, and he thought he detected a note of exasperation.

"It's sweet. It's thoughtful. And it's suffocating."

"Why don't you tell them?"

"Ha! As if I haven't tried. Totally pointless. They've made up their minds, and actually I don't know what I'd do without them. However, I do what I want and just let them think it was their idea." She smiled. "Keeps everyone happy."

"I know that my research still has some flaws," Marcus began as he eased the El Dorado into the rush-hour New York traffic. "But they'll be worked out. I believe what I'm doing."

"I know you do. I hear the passion in your voice whenever you speak about your work."

"Deanna, when I read about your accident—I know this may sound crazy—but you became a personal crusade for me. Working toward a cure to restore your vision gave me the incentive that I was missing in my work. And in my life." He dared to snatch a look at her. She had her hand folded in her lap, her head held high, her expression unreadable. "I felt that so much was lost when you lost your sight, and I wanted to do something to change that. The work, the research, everything has been driven by you."

Did he dare tell her everything? That since his wife's death two years earlier nothing had mattered to him? Christine was his world and when she left it, his seemed to end. He couldn't concentrate on his work, he fell behind on his reports, funders threatened to hold back their support, and there was near anarchy among his research team. And then he'd read about Deanna, and something within him started to bloom. She so reminded his of his Chris, beautiful, full of life and energy at the height of a brilliant medical career, when tragedy struck in the dorm of a drunk driver. Deanna gave him a reason to put his life back on track. No, she didn't need to know that, at least not now.

She lowered her head, her long, slim fingers entwined on her lap. "Marcus...I'm honored, flattered, and humbled to think that even though you didn't know me you felt compelled by my...situation." She angled her head toward him. "But I think you need to be honest with yourself and me. I may be a reason for your research, but there's more to it than that. If your technique is successful it won't matter who it's successful on, just that it is. You want my name attached to it."

"But—"

"Admit it, because it's true. And I don't have a problem with that. What I do have a problem with is your lack of honesty." She smiled. "Because I can't read the expression on your face doesn't mean I can't sense the struggle that's going on in you."

Her tone wasn't admonishing or belligerent, Marcus realized, but accepting and quite matter of fact. And she was right. She seemed to read his motives as flawlessly as she scaled the piano keys.

He pulled up to a red light. "What can I say? You're right, or at least in part."

"In part?"

A car horn blared impatiently behind them, and he made the turn onto Columbus Circle.

"Yes." He hoped that what he was about to confess wouldn't scare her away totally. "Over the past year or more, I ...you became my central focus. Yes, part of it was because of your name and the validity it would give my work." He swallowed. "The other reason is a lot more personal."

Slowly he began to tell her about Christine, their three-year marriage and their crushed plans for the future. "After Christine was killed, I was just a shell. I didn't have any reason for getting up in the morning. Until you."

His gaze darted briefly toward her, and he caught the subtle shift in her body. "I became enchanted by you, Deanna, by everything about you. Your talent entertained me, your generosity toward others touched me, and your beauty captured my heart." He knew he sounded like a love-struck teen, but he couldn't seem to stem the flow of words that had been bottled up for so long.

"Marcus...I..."

"I know." He chuckled, disconcerted by his revelation. "We've lived thousands of miles apart. I'd never met you until recently. But I have now, Deanna, and nothing has changed. If anything, meeting you has only cemented everything I've been feeling." His heart was thundering and he could feel the trickle of nervous perspiration on his back.

"I don't know what to say."

"Don't say anything. Just think about it. Not just the operation, but everything else. I do have to return to London. My work, my life is there. I only ask that while I'm here, we could spend some time together. And maybe you'll even visit me in London."

He pulled into a space several doors down from her house. She turned in her seat, sought and found his hand, taking them into hers.

"Marcus, I hope that we will always remain friends. No matter what happens. I can't offer you, or promise more than that."

"Is it because of Clay?"

"Yes." Her answer was clear, devoid of hesitation.

"I can offer you so much, Deanna. I can offer you the chance to see again. How can you so easily dismiss it?" He squeezed her hand. "If you can't accept me, then at least accept my skills as a surgeon."

He saw the struggle dance across her features, the instant of hesitation. He thought he saw an opening and took it. "Don't you want to look out your window and see the leaves on the trees turn from green to red to gold? Watch flocks of birds fly South for the winter, see snow pile up on the gray concrete, waves lapping against sandy beaches?"

"Stop it! Just stop it." She snatched her hand from his grasp. "I don't want to hear anymore." She shook her head. "You don't understand."

"Then tell me," he urged. "Tell me why you want to stay in a world of darkness, hiding in the private arena you've created?"

"Maybe this is where I want to be. Maybe I'm happy, content, fulfilled for the first time in my life."

"Are you?"

This time she did hesitate, but only for a beat. "Yes. I am."

He took a long, deep breath. "Deanna, I'm sorry. I had no right to push you like that. It's just that—"

"You want to give me something that you think I need." She reached out and gently explored his face. A soft smile curved her mouth. "I'll always be grateful for that. I want us to stay friends, and I sincerely want you to continue your research and perfect your technique. I'll help you in any way I can, through the Foundation," she added, her voice as gentle as her fingertips gliding across his face.

He clasped her hand and held them against his cheeks. "If you ever change your mind…"

"I won't," she whispered.

He stayed in New York for another month before returning to London. During that time, he visited Deanna at the Institute, shared dinner with her at her house on several occasions, and even convinced her to have a traditional African dinner at a cozy little restaurant in Brooklyn the night before he was scheduled to return to London.

"Thank you for tonight," he said afterward on the top step of her home while a stirring fall breeze rustled around them, blowing strands of her hair across her face. He reached out and tucked the wayward tendrils behind her ear, then gently removed the dark glasses she had put on before entering the restaurant.

She ducked her head, and he tilted it upward with a fingertip.

"I'm going to miss you very much, Deanna. This past month meant a great deal to me."

She didn't respond.

"Will you write?"

She grinned suddenly. "Can't promise that. But I will call. Collect."

"As long as you do."

"Have a safe flight, Marcus."

"I'll call you." He leaned down and gently brushed her forehead with his mouth. He wanted to linger. He wanted to taste her lips, just once, and hold her body tight against his. He knew he shouldn't. But he did, before she could stop him, cupping her chin and lowering his mouth to meld with hers. Just for a moment. It was all the time he needed.

He eased back before she had the chance to react, turned, and walked away.

That was more than a year ago. A year since he'd seen her, and though they kept in touch by phone, the calls became less frequent over time.

He thought of her constantly and wondered if she thought of him, of the kiss they'd shared. But they never talked about that last night.

He kept her abreast of his work, and a month ago he'd received sanction from the AMA to try his procedure. That was when he'd received the letter from Deanna asking him to be here tonight, at Radio City Music Hall.

And so here he was in one of the most famous buildings in New York City. One of hundreds who had come to pay tribute to an incredible woman.

His pulse raced when the President ended his short speech and the spotlight focused once again on the emcee, who began his prepackaged acknowledgments while the music from Deanna's last CD, *Turning Point*, played in the background.

The spotlight panned the audience and settled on Deanna. A closed-circuit picture of her seated in the audience with Tracy loomed on the screen.

A wave of renewed excitement rippled through the audience. The long, if entertaining, wait for their princess would soon be over. Marcus, too, held his breath. Waited and wondered.

CHAPTER XVI

"Well, sis, are you ready to face your public?" Tracy squeezed Deanna's hand. "This is your moment."

Deanna's smile wavered ever so slightly. She leaned toward Tracy and whispered, "I knew this moment was coming. I must have rehearsed what I was going to say a million times. But Trace, at this moment, I can't remember my own name."

Tracy had a giggle behind her hand. "Then just do what everybody else does: Thank God, their mothers, and their producers!"

"Girl, you are too crazy."

"But it's true."

"Don't I know it," Deanna whispered, settling back in her seat.

She tried to listen to the words, hear the music, but everything started to blend together into one kaleidoscopic ball of music and light.

What would she say? What could she say that would begin to express the depth of her gratitude, or help all those watching to understand why she'd made the choices she did?

At times, even she didn't understand. But in her heart she knew she was doing, and had done, the right thing.

From the moment she walked in on Cord and his lover, she felt her world take an unmistakable turn. She had to reach deep inside herself to find strength and pride, and move on. She didn't realize then just how much she would need those resources she'd uncovered within herself. Just thinking about those days after she left California still sent the needles of reality pricking at her defenses. Whatever naiveté she'd had was vanquished in the blink of an eye.

Funny, but she'd made the trip to California to break things off with Cord. She had been apprehensive, afraid— and he'd made it so easy. Musing on it, she let the memories envelope her, sweeping her back.

California

Calling first was out of the question. Although thinking back now, I should have. My flight from New York landed at LAX about ten o'clock on a Friday night. Cord's beach house was about twenty minutes away, barring traffic, which was always in a state of gridlock.

Anyway, the cab ride, which turned into a forty-five minute marathon, gave me some time to get my farewell speech together. I knew it wasn't going to be easy, but it was something I should have done a long time ago. I'd never had the nerve, and foolishly thought that the way things were between Cord and me were just the way they were supposed to be.

I guess the final straw came when I'd returned home to Connecticut from my tour and Tracy stopped by for a visit and saw the bruises. I was just so happy to be home after traveling for months, the first thing I did when I got in was jump into a hot sudsy tub of water, then changed into my favorite pair of cut-off denim shorts and scoop-necked T-shirt. When the bell rang, I wasn't even thinking.

"Tracy!"

"Hey girl." She squeezed me in her trademark bear hug and I couldn't help but flinch, my body still aching from my night with Cord.

She moved back and took a long look at me. Suddenly I felt hot.

"What's with the bruises on your neck?" Her eyes rolled down my body. "And on your thighs?"

I couldn't meet her stare.

"What's going on, Dee? This isn't the first time I've noticed. But it's the last time I'm going to keep my mouth shut." She walked down the step into the living room and put a bag of Chinese food on the table.

"It's nothing," I mumbled, trying real hard to sound cavalier.

"Nothing! Those bruises on your neck and your thighs look like something to me. Did Cord do this, Dee?" She planted her hands on her hips and waited for my answer.

"It's not what you think." My mind was spinning. How could I explain something that I didn't understand? My mother didn't prepare me. We never had those conversations. Hours of rehearsal consumed my free time and negated any possibility of forming relationships. Not that many girls wanted to befriend me. With my mixed racial background, I never looked like the other girls and always felt insecure, not knowing where I fit. Most of them were either ambivalent, believing that I thought I was better than they were because I was shy and kept to myself, or they ignored me altogether. And now at twenty-eight, I felt stupid having to reveal just how inexperienced I was.

I plopped down in my favorite overstuffed chair, and Tracy sat opposite me on the love seat.

"Talk to me, Dee."

"I don't know where to begin."

"How about starting with the fact that I'm your friend and you can tell me anything?"

She waited and stalled. But at the same time I knew that Tracy had determination to match and surpass mine. She'd sit right there until doomsday, or until she got an answer. Whichever came first.

I struggled, halting, rambling through a story I had never told another person. All my fears, my shame, poured out in a sudden rush of words. I relived all the moments between Cord and me, the good and the dark times. The times when his own weaknesses, the cracks in his personality spread and grew, striking out at me, the person closest to him.

"I know...I should have left him, but in the beginning when he first started getting...aggressive, I just thought it was the way things were supposed to be...I...he was the first man I'd ever been with, Tracy. I...thought that was just the way things were."

Tracy reached across the short space that separated us and took my hand. "Dee, sex, love, making love between a man and a woman isn't supposed to hurt. It's not supposed to cause you pain, or make you feel ashamed. Cord is taking his pain, his frustrations, and his insecurities out on you. That's not healthy."

"I wanted to help him. I wanted him to see someone, but he refused. I know a lot of what he's going through is because of his relationship with his father."

"But, Dee, you've got to understand *you* can't help Cord. He needs more than what you can offer him. You need to let him go, make room in your life for a man who will care for you like the treasure you are."

"A part of me always knew that, but I felt that if I left him…" I tried to collect my thoughts. I knew I wasn't making any sense. "Before I met Cord, I had no life, Tracy. You know that. He showed me how to enjoy it…at least most of the time."

"But at what cost?"

I knew she was right. I'd allowed my own need to be needed to blind me to the fact that I was hurting inside and was too afraid to make changes, afraid of being alone again.

I'd heard about Cord's affairs. I'd dealt with his mood swings and his rough sex. But beneath it all, I believed, and always would, that Cord truly cared about me, in the only way he knew how.

"You've got to let go, Dee. For your own sake. For Cord's sake."

I slept on what Tracy'd said. I re-ran in my mind the two years of my relationship with Cord like a filmstrip, reliving the good and bad times. I wasn't happy with what I saw. I guess I never wanted more than what I had because something inside me didn't believe I deserved more. But I did. Of course, I did. Everyone deserved to be happy, and I had to find a way to get my own happiness. Whatever that was.

Two nights later I was on a plane bound for Los Angeles. I could have taken the easy way out and written a "Dear Cord" letter or hidden behind the telephone. If I was going to make changes in my life, I had to do it the right way, even if it was the hard way.

The cab dropped me off at the end of the pebbled drive, and I told the driver to wait.

The house was dark, save for the lights on the deck. At first I thought Cord wasn't home, but as I walked up the path I saw his Jaguar parked by the side of the house. It didn't matter, he never locked the doors anyway. If he wasn't home, I'd made up my mind that I would just wait.

I walked around the side of the house and slid open the glass door. I turned on the living room light, and that was when I heard muffled sounds coming from the back.

"Cord."

No answer.

Stupidly—just like in those movies I hated with the idiot woman who goes toward the noises instead of away from them—I continued down the hallway, barely noticing the stark white walls adorned with priceless works of art by Monet, Renoir, and Van Gogh. Cord never spared any expense when it came to his creature comforts and discriminating tastes.

The bedroom door at the end of the hall was partially open. As I came closer, the muffled noises I'd heard grew louder. I looked down and saw a wet towel and a pair of swim trunks balled in a heap on the floor.

My breath seemed to stick in my throat and my heart was beating like frantically flapping wings. I knew what I was going to find. At least I thought I did. I should have turned around. Should have just left it alone. But I didn't. I walked right up to that door and pushed it open, sure that I was going to see Cord tangled up with some starlet.

At first they didn't hear me. They were too engrossed in what they were doing. I just stood there, my insides diving and twisting like a boat tossed about during a violent storm. Something made Cord turn. Maybe it was the gasp that I thought I'd captured behind my hand, or maybe it was the light the hallway that washed into the room like a finger accusation.

Pure terror lighted Cord's onyx eyes, only surpassed by the shock in the eyes of the man beneath him.

My voice seemed to come from some alien depth. I barely recognized it as my own. "I came to tell you it was over between us, Cord," I said with a calm that frightened me. "But you've already taken care of that."

I thought I heard him call my name, but my head was pounding so hard I couldn't be sure, and I didn't care. I closed the door, walked out, and never turned back.

On the flight home, through the night and into the next day, I vacillated between denial, self-recrimination, and outrage. It was obvious, I kept telling myself, that I'd been seeing things. *Not Cord.* Not Mr. Macho, Mr. Ladies' Man.

I shifted from denial to the painful level, the what's-wrong-with-me syndrome, and questioned my femininity. Maybe I was the reason our sex life was so unfulfilling— because of me, he sought his satisfaction elsewhere. Maybe it was because of me that he'd become so rough and callous. And underlying that mental and emotional roller coaster was a layer of anger that burned and scorched my insides like a flame left to smolder in the folds of a mattress, then suddenly exploding in a blaze.

I threw things. I ranted and raved. I smoked cigarettes for the first time in my life and slept not knowing or caring if it was day or night. By the time I paid attention to myself again, I realized I was still in the same clothes I'd worn to California. I tore them off, wrapped them in a bundle, put on my terry-cloth robe, took the bundle out to the garbage, dumped it, and set it on fire. I stood there like some dazed pyromaniac, watching the flames devour my past. Whiffs of smoke billowed upward, and it was then that the dam finally burst, and I cried. Wailed. Deep, wracking sobs, and not because I was devastated and betrayed, though I was, but because I was actually happy. I was free. The deep burden of guilt and feelings of inadequacy rode along with the clouds of smoke, dissipating into the air.

And throughout my entire three-day ordeal, Cord constantly called, leaving pleading messages on my machine, begging me to listen, wanting me to understand that what I saw had nothing to do with me—with us. He even swore he'd go to counseling if I would just pick up the phone and listen to him.

Finally I snatched up the phone, too tired to hear any more sorrow being inflicted on my innocent machine.

"Cord, only you can decide what you want to do with your life and with whom. I didn't break it off with you because of what I saw, but because of what I need for me. For once, I'll always be thankful to you for the happy times you brought into my life. But I need to move on for my own well-being. You can continue to go through life taking out your anger and pain about your father on everyone who comes near you, or you can finally do something positive about it."

I took a long breath, feeling the waves of relief and anxiety wash through me, cleanse me. "Please don't call me anymore, Cord. I'd really appreciate it if you didn't."

"Deanna, please, please don't leave me. I need you."

I almost believed him. Three days ago, I would have. "No, you don't, Cord. Good-bye."

"Dee, wait."

"Yes?"

"You won't tell, will you?"

I almost laughed. How typical. "Good-bye, Cord."

I hung up the phone, determined to put that part of my life behind me. Thinking about it now, I was an easy conquest for Cord. I'd spent my whole life being dictated to, directed and controlled. So I couldn't blame him or myself. We were both being who we were. We both need to change.

CHAPTER XVII

I finally pulled myself together, cleaned up the mess I'd made in my house, and returned Tracy's one hundredth phone call.

"Girl, where have you been? I was a hot minute away from calling 911."

"And hello to you, too," I replied, glad to hear her voice, even though I knew she was going to interrogate me, and had every right to.

Tracy and I were close. Closer than most blood sisters. We looked out for each other, and when one was hurt or suffering, the other shared the pain. I understood her anxiety. I would have reacted the same way had the roles been reversed. She did deserve an explanation.

"Yeah, yeah, hello. Now are you going to tell me where you've been? You had me worried sick."

"Tracy, I took a trip to LA."

"Oh…yeah."

I didn't miss the cautious edge to her voice. "I saw Cord." *Did I ever.* "I told him it was over."

"And…how did he take it?"

"I think he was shocked, to say the least."

"How are you? Really?"

"I'm okay. Better, actually."

"You did the right thing, Dee. Believe that. It'll get easier with time."

"I'm sure it will."

"Is there something you're not telling me, Deanna? I just have this feeling there's more to this than you're saying."

For a moment I thought about telling her everything, my shock, my hurt, my questions about my womanhood. But I didn't. That last scene, Cord's and my final curtain, would never be reviewed by anyone else. If I owed Cord nothing else, I would keep his secret safe.

And for the first time in our decade-long friendship, I lied. "I guess I'm just tired, Trace. I think I'll go riding tomorrow. Get some fresh air and clear my head."

"Sounds good. Maybe I'll stop by tomorrow evening. I'll bring Chinese."

"You'd better!"

The following morning was just the kind of day fairy tales were made of. The sky was a soft, clear blue, with gentle puffs of clouds dotting the heavens. The warm sun played a game of hide-and-seek, ducking behind the clouds and popping out to spread its warmth.

Spring was always my favorite time of the year, when everything was new, fresh, like starting over.

I rolled down the car windows, inhaling the distinctive aroma of budding flowers and green grass as I drove along the stretch of the highway to the stables. The music from the car stereo floated around me, drawing me in. I settled back against the soft leather headrest just as I spotted the stables up ahead.

Parking the car, I stepped out and took a deep breath of pungent air. The mixture of fresh earth, hay, and horses all blended together into a unique aroma. Hmm. There was nothing like it.

I strolled across the hard-packed dirt road that led to the main house, waving and smiling at all the familiar faces. Growing up, when I wasn't behind the piano, I was here at the stables, racing like the wind across the terrain, forgetting the pressures and demands of my life. I composed some of my best work—in my head—while riding Dreammaker.

By the time I reached her stall, Dreammaker was already harnessed and ready. After our customary nose-nuzzling and my stroking of her mane, I led her outside.

"Keep your head to the sky, Ms. Winters," Jake, one of the stable hands, warned over a jawful of snuff. "'Spose to kick up a storm out there. You know that horse of yours don't like the thunder."

"Sky looks clear to me, Jake. But I'll keep it in mind."

"You do that now," he mumbled, moving onto the next stall with his trademark bowlegged shuffle.

I led Dreammaker out of the stable and onto the riding trail, all the while catching her up on my travels since the last time I'd seen her. I even whispered in her ear about the scene at Cord's beach house. And if I didn't know better, I'd swear she took it to heart. She furiously shook her large black head and snorted he outrage. I had to laugh.

"Don't take it so hard, girl. I'm almost over it."

She whinnied in response.

We started off with a slow trot, getting reacquainted, then gradually picked up the pace until we were racing together, as one unit, as we were meant to.

We leapt hurdles, darted over narrow streams, sped past huge oak trees. My heart was racing as fast as we were. The adrenaline rush pounded in my ears like waves crashing against the rocky shore. I felt as if I could fly, with the wind whipping against my face, pressing against my body.

Everything was magnified in intensity, the twittering and shrilling of birds, colors in a neon glow, the drumbeat of hooves as loud as distant thunder. My heart, my spirit, my nature, seemed to blend together into one gigantic sphere of white light at the exact moment that Dreammaker rose on her hind legs, seeming to fight off some unseen enemy, her blood-chilling scream renting the air.

And then everything was black.

CHAPTER XVIII

Sounds. Voices were muffled, as if my ears were stuffed with cotton balls. They came from somewhere around me, but I couldn't figure it out. I felt disoriented, as if I were caught in an underwater dream. I tried to struggle to the surface, break over the waves, but I couldn't move. And every inch of me throbbed with pain.

I had to wake up. This dream scared me. Why was it so dark? I always leave the light on in the hall. The bulb must have blown.

Something was wrong. The smells, the sounds, were not from my house. *Antiseptic.* I wasn't at home.

Panic gripped me. I couldn't breathe. The dream, this dark underwater nightmare, was sucking me in, holding onto my arms, my legs. Oh, God. I couldn't breathe.

"Ms. Winters. Ms. Winters. Please, take it easy."

It was a woman's voice, but I didn't recognize it. Gentle hands pressed against my aching shoulders. Why couldn't I see the hands? The hands were pushing me back down into the dream. I had to get out.

Strange, strangled sounds filled my ears, and then I realized that they came from me.

"Ms. Winters. You've been in an accident. You're in the hospital. Please try to relax."

I tried to breathe...in...out.

"The doctor will be right in. He'll explain everything."

Moments later I heard a voice on my left. I tried to turn, but a stampede of pain in my head went wild.

"Don't try to move, Ms. Winters. I'm Dr. Larkin. Do you remember anything about what happened?"

"Why can't I see?" My voice was a croak. "Why can't I move?"

"Let's tackle one thing at a time."

I heard metal scraping against the floor and assumed he was pulling a chair closer to the bed. Gently he lifted my head and placed a plastic cup against my dry lips. Water dropped across them and down my throat.

"You were in a riding accident, Ms. Winters." He eased me back down on the pillow. "Three weeks ago. You were thrown from your horse during a lightning storm. You sustained extensive head and internal injuries."

I tried to remember. It was all such a blur. "How bad?" My voice still sounded like a cat's claws scratching against wood.

"We had to operate to stop the internal bleeding."

I felt the rush again, as if I'd been running for miles and couldn't catch my breath. "Just tell…me," I croaked, but I didn't really want to hear what he had to say.

"Your head injuries caused bone fragments to damage your eyes."

"My…eyes?"

I felt his hand suddenly on mine. I didn't want him to touch me, this messenger of doom, but I couldn't pull away.

"We won't know for sure. We'll have to wait until we can take the bandages off."

"We won't know what for sure?" My heart was going to explode.

"We won't know if you'll be able to see when we remove the bandages."

If I concentrated really hard, I knew I could keep myself from screaming, and if I focused, I could make myself breathe in and out and slow down my heart before it jumped out of my chest.

They were just guessing. They weren't sure. Doctors never know anything, anyway. They always wanted to give you the worst-case scenario. Just in case. Of course I would see again. He was just being paranoid.

"And what else?"

"You won't be able to have children, Ms. Winters. I'm sorry."

"Does…anyone…know…I'm here?"

"Ms. Moore is right outside. She's been here day and night."

I swallowed, hoping that what I was about to say would go back down, but didn't. "Please…tell her…to go home."

CHAPTER XIX

"Just leave me alone, Tracy. Do you understand? Leave me alone!"

"For the past two months, you've been telling me the same crap. Dee, you can't spend the rest of your life in bed. The doctors said you need to go into therapy. You have to learn to take care of yourself."

"Take care of myself. Ha. That's real funny, Trace. You mean tap, tap, tapping with a cane, being led through the street by a dog? Is that what you mean?"

I knew I was being cruel. I knew I was taking my pain out on her. But damnit, life had dealt me a nasty blow. Cruel and unusual punishment—for what, I still didn't know. My prayers pleaded for my sight back and when that failed, I asked for understanding. Why? What did I do to deserve losing my sight and the ability to bring life into the world? What horrible thing had I done? Why have you forsaken me?

But I didn't get an answer from up above. And no one here on earth had an explanation either. Other than "it was just a tragic accident."

Yeah, real tragic.

So what else could I do but take my hurt out on the one person closest to me? She'd just have to understand, or she could go straight to hell with all the rest of my shattered dreams.

I turned over on my side and curled my knees up to my chest.

"Deanna."

She was talking to my back, but I didn't care. I just wanted to go to sleep, wake up, and realize that this was one long phantasm.

"You're being discharged tomorrow, Dee, whether you like it or not. You're going home."

I felt those damned tears start to form, burning pools in my eyes. I cried a lot lately. But only when no one was looking. Before I wound up in the hospital, the last time I remembered crying was when I fell out of my tree house and broke my arm. I was about eight. Twenty years ago; I hadn't time for tears since then. As a matter of fact, they weren't allowed. My folks thought they were just excuses to get out of doing something I didn't want, or worse, not performing up to what standard was expected.

So I didn't cry. I just worked harder. Now I didn't even have that. So here were those damned tears. I bit down on my lip to hold them back. The last thing I needed was for someone to feel sorry for me. Even Tracy. Especially Tracy.

"I'll be here to pick you up."

I didn't answer. I couldn't. Going home, leaving this secure, sterile fortress of my guardrailed bed, simply terrified me.

I suppose it was the next day, because when I woke up again I smelled those powdered eggs that impersonated the real thing and heard the cling-clang of the food cart rattling down the hospital corridor.

I sat up, expecting a nurse to bring my breakfast. Instead I heard a bevy of urgent whispers and poorly stifled giggles. My heart suddenly jolted with recognition when a familiar scent drifted toward my bed.

"C-Cord?"

His essence enveloped me, and then I felt a whisper of a kiss brush my forehead. He combed my tousled hair away from my face with his fingertips.

"Forgive me, Deanna," he whispered, his voice seeming to come from the depths of his soul. He took my hand and pressed it to his lips. "I should have come long ago. I would have. You know that. But the last time..." His voice drifted, and I heard him draw in a long breath. "I didn't think you'd want to see me."

I squeezed his hand back because I couldn't find any words to say. I knew what it took for him to come. Cord might be vain, self-centered, and possibly self-destructive, but he was a man of great pride. And I knew that was the reason why his father's inattentiveness wounded him so deeply.

"I'm glad...you came." I could feel the tension slowly ease from his body, as if those simple words had soothed him.

I heard a chair scrape on the floor as he pulled it toward the bed and sat beside me.

"Hmm, *chica*, you deserve much better surroundings than this drab hovel. I thought I taught you better."

I couldn't imagine what he saw, but knowing Cord, if it wasn't up to the standards of the Ritz, it was a dump. I could almost see his aristocratic nose turned down in disappointment.

"It doesn't matter. I can't see it anyway." I didn't even try to keep the bitterness out of my voice.

"*Si*. This is true. And what are you going to do about it? I talked with your doctors, *Preciosa*. They say you refuse rehabilitation. You won't even get out of your bed. Not only will you be blind and disheveled, you'll be fat!"

He sputtered the words out with such total incredulity that I couldn't help but smile.

And then I laughed. From the bottom of my toes, I laughed. I laughed until my stomach ached and water squeezed from my eyes. And we held each other.

"I needed that," I said sniffling and hiccupping.

"So did I, Deanna."

For a few moments we just sat. Quiet. Not talking. Holding hands. I guess he was thinking about the good times too. At least I hoped he was.

"I've started counseling," he said, pulling me away from my thoughts.

"You have? Oh, Cord, I'm so happy for you. How is it?"

"Hard. Probably the hardest thing I've ever done. But it's helping. I think."

"It will take time. Stick with it."

"It was because of you that I went." He stroked my hand. "That's why I'm here now." He leaned closer. I could feel his minty breath graze my cheek. "You musn't do this to yourself, Deanna. You are so much better, so much more than you are allowing yourself to become. I know relearning your life will be painful, the most painful thing you've ever done. I know, because it is for me. When I met you, you were this innocent, inexperienced girl-woman. When you walked in on me, you were a woman in control with no regrets. What happened to her?"

"Her life got snatched out from under her. That's what happened."

"Then snatch it back! What did I tell you about money, fame, and the pleasure that they can afford you? *Que?*"

"That…if you have them…use them."

"Exactly!" he shouted, as if impressed with a slow student who'd finally gotten the answer right. "Then use them. Use what you have to get the best care, the best doctors, the best thereapists, your name and your money can buy. Use them to make a life you can live in. One that you deserve, that you have control over."

He took a deep breath, and I realized that he was standing. His voice seemed to envelope me. "Or you can spend the rest of your days being a pitiful burden on society. That, my dear Deanna, would be the greatest tragedy of all."

In all the time that I'd known Cord, I truly believe that was the first instance when he was sincerely, without equivocation, concerned about someone else. Yes, it's true Cord had the capacity to love, but he focused so much of his energy on himself and satisfying his own needs, he rarely had anything left to offer another person. If you understood that about him, you could understand that Cord Herrera was a hurt little boy who spent his time, energy, and money trying to stop the pain.

To have him come to me and show that rare side of himself touched me in a way nothing else had.

"Think about it, *mi amore*." I felt his lips press against my cheek, and then he was gone.

When Tracy arrived to take me home, a nurse helped me into the chair and pushed me down the busy hallway. Cord's words came rushing back, and I knew then that I couldn't live the rest of my life strapped in a wheelchair. Or being led around, be it by man or beast.

"Wait."

We came to an abrupt halt.

"What?" Tracy asked. "Did you forget something?"

"Yes." I swallowed back the last of my qualms. "Before we go, would you mind getting the name of that rehabilitation center in New York?" I could almost see the smile splitting Tracy's face.

"Hey, sis, not to worry." She patted my shoulder. "I don't leave home without it. Let's roll! No pun intended." She giggled, and so did I.

CHAPTER XX

Going home was hard. It was as if I'd stepped into a foreign country where I didn't understand the language of the terrain. The house I'd lived in for almost eight years could just as easily have been an Egyptian pyramid for all the recognition I had of it.

I can't count the number of times I bumped my shins, overflowed a glass, or ate under- or overcooked food. Until the arrival of my housekeeper—whom Tracy insisted I hire—I confined myself to eating sandwiches. And who knows what my outfits must have looked like.

I think it was about the third day that I was home—and the housekeeper had to put out a small fire because I dropped a towel on a hot burner—that I made up my mind to start over. There was no way that I could put off going into therapy any longer.

"I want to move to New York, Tracy," I said when she arrived to pay her nightly "check up on Deanna" visit.

"Move? What on earth for? The doctors at the rehabilitation said you could live at the facility for as long as you need and then go home. I'd come up and visit every weekend."

I heard the alarm in her voice and realized that this major upheaval would be just as hard on her as it was on me. We were practically joined at the hip. Tracy's parents died when she was fifteen, and she was raised by her aunt, who wasn't the most nurturing person in the world.

When Tracy and I met, it was a match made in heaven. She, with her tough, aggressive personality, and me...well, me being who I was, we clicked. And now I was telling her I was severing the tie that bound us.

"I need to do this. I feel that an entire change in environment is what I need to start this new life of mine. There are just too many memories here."

"But, Dee, everything that's familiar to you is here. Your friends. Your studio. The stables."

"That part of my life is behind me. I won't ever ride again. And as for my music, well, I have no intention of playing in front of an audience. Going into the recording studio is the farthest thing from my mind. I need to work on me for a while."

I held out my hand and she took it. "As for friend, you're the only friend I have. And no matter where we are, that's never going to change."

"You're determined to do this?"

"Absolutely."

I heard her sigh and desperately wished I could see her face.

"What can I do to help?"

"I thought you'd never ask."

For the first month, I lived at the residence provided by the center, which was located on the Upper East Side of Manhattan. The move wasn't as traumatic as I'd imagined. I think the comfort came from knowing there were others like me who were struggling to take their places in the world. What was difficult was the grueling hours of training and rehab. We had to relearn how to function, using every sense save the one of sight. We had cooking and computer classes. We learned how to organize our money, our clothes, and do laundry. Learning Braille and mastering maneuvering from one point to the next were top priorities.

I think during my stay there, my years of single-minded training and striving for perfection paid off in an entirely new way. I actually began to look forward to the next day and the new challenges it presented.

My greatest challenge came after I'd been at the center for about three months, and I was approached by Dr. St. Claire. It was my turn to prepare the evening meal for the six other residents in my wing. We'd just finished dinner when he approached my table.

"Deanna. How are you this evening?"

I turned toward the sound of the calming, familiar voice and smiled. He was my favorite therapist, but a relentless instructor.

"How are you, doctor? Have you had dinner?"

"As a matter of fact, I have. I understand you prepared it. You did an excellent job."

"Thanks. It's getting easier. I think."

"Everything gets easier over time and with practice. I've been watching your progress. You're doing extremely well. I think you'll be ready to leave us soon."

A sudden wave of panic gripped me as surely as if someone had taken their hands and wrapped them around my throat. Even though Tracy had found a house for me, as I'd wanted, and was getting it furnished, the thought of leaving totally rattled me.

"I...don't think I'm ready. Not yet."

He patted my hand. "Of course you are. Everyone who comes here feels that way when the time comes."

"Do you really think I am? I feel there's so much I don't know. Things I'm unsure of."

"We've taught you all we can, Deanna. Now you have to go out into the real world and use it."

But I was afraid. Afraid to go back into the world that had never been kind to me. Afraid that all the people I could not see would be whispering and pointing at me, waiting for me to make a mistake. I was fearful that outside of this sanctuary I would be different. Tears of fear burned my eyes and threatened to overflow.

Dr. St. Claire must have seen what I fought to hide. His hand was suddenly covering mine.

"Come. Let's go to my office. There's something I want to discuss with you."

Once inside his office, he helped me to a seat.

"Deanna," he began in that soothing voice that could lull a raging storm. "I've studied your case very carefully and read all of your test results. I've watched you these past months and observed your persistence, your determination. You have a natural instinct to strive for perfection. And because of that I believe you would be the right candidate for a technique I've been working on."

I felt my heart knock against my chest and that sudden wave of exhilaration that you get when you anticipate good news, tightened my stomach. He was going to give me my sight back.

I let go of a shaky breath. "Tell me. What is it?"

He pulled his chair closer. I could feel his nearness.

"According to all of your tests, you can still make out shapes."

I swallowed. "Barely. Everything seems submerged in blankets of darkness. Sometimes I think what I see is just my imagination. I can pinpoint where someone is, but that's about it."

"That's all you need. I want you to begin our sensory program. From all of my observations of you, I get the impression that your greatest fear is feeling and being perceived as different, someone to feel sorry for you. You need a challenge, Deanna. That's why you drive yourself the way you do, and, I believe, to the exclusion of everything else. Am I right?"

"It was that way for most of my life. Then for a while, it wasn't." And that digression, that time with Cord, had changed me. I trusted him with my heart and my body, and he betrayed both. Even though, in my heart, I'd put that episode behind me, the scars were still there, buried beneath the surface. I could never allow anyone to get that close to me again. Ever.

But who would want me now, anyway?

The pain of that realization told me exactly what I needed to know. I must put my all, my everything, into myself. Before the accident it was my music, my riding, my fans, my instructors, Cord. With all that behind me, I would use everything I had to perfecting my life in a dark, colorless world.

"Tell me about the program, Dr. St. Claire, and what I need to do."

For the first six weeks, Dr. St. Claire worked with me every day for six hours. I endured a battery of coordination and memory exercises. I began to learn how to move gracefully from a room without the aid of a cane by tightly focusing, in my mind, on precisely where everything was located. I took "touch" sessions, and I began to develop the ability to determine fabrics and surfaces by how they felt.

The most difficult task to master was appearing to see without being able to see. I had to learn to determine the distance and height of a person's voice and allow my senses to pick up body heat to estimate how close someone was to me. I became the perfect flirt, according to Dr. St. Claire, when I would keep my gaze lowered until I could put together all the details I needed to "see" someone, and then I'd slowly look up.

"Deanna," Dr. St. Claire said toward the end of the sixth week, "you are absolutely astounding. I've never had a student who actually absorbed everything around them. There's nothing more I can teach you, my dear. You are ready."

I doubted that I was ready, but I moved into my new house with Tracy's help. Within two weeks I had every bit of furniture, clothing, and food product exactly where I wanted it. I was able to move around my house without mishap and was actually beginning to feel good about myself again.

We were sitting in my living room one Saturday evening, listening to some music and drinking coffee, when Tracy made a revelation that completely changed the direction of my life.

"Dee, since the accident you've been receiving tons of mail. I didn't want to bother you with it before, but now—well, since you're home and settled—I guess you can decide what you want to do."

"I guess I can start sending out thank you cards or something."

"I think you're going to have to do a lot more than that, girlfriend."

"What do you mean?"

"Well, according to my last count, and that's not including this week's mail, you've received checks, money orders, and cash totaling one hundred and fifty thousand dollars."

"What!"

"You heard me. And the money keeps coming in. The doctors want you to know how much you're cared about."

"Tracy, I can't keep that money. I've made enough money to take care of myself for the rest of my life."

"Then you need to think about what you're going to do."

And that's how the Deanna Winters Foundation was born. I didn't need the money, but there were countless others who did. I had a purpose again. A reason why.

CHAPTER XXI

Getting the Deanna Winters Foundation off the ground was one of the great moments in my life. Not only did it give me a purpose, a reason for being, but I think it finally helped me to understand that I was meant for something more than just being an entertainer.

I remembered Cord's words, "Use your money to make a life that you can live." And that's what I did. With Tracy's help, of course.

She gave up her job at the law firm in Connecticut, moved down to New York, and opened a small office where we handled Foundation business. The Foundation opened without a lot of fanfare. I wanted to remain as far out of the limelight as possible. The goal of the Foundation was not to bring attention to me but to the causes of the visually impaired. Within several months of opening, we were giving away money for research and to assist rehab centers. We received tons of letters from all over the world asking for our help. Most of them came from parents requesting help for their children. That's what gave us our direction.

However, as much as I didn't want to have to face people, I forced myself to make the necessary trips to meet some of our generous donors. It was during one of my infrequent trips about a year after the Foundation was operational, that Clay McDaniels was mentioned by one of our donors.

"Find out everything you can about Mr. McDaniels," I told Tracy on our flight back from Senegal. "If he's as good as we've been told, his help would be welcome. These trips, even though they're necessary, are very difficult for me."

"I know," she said, squeezing my hand. "But when some people give their money away they want to put a face to the cause."

I laughed. "I wish I could say the same thing. At least if we had someone we could trust to handle the transactions and the travel, we could focus more on what our goals are for the Foundation and start making plans to get the Institute up and running. We certainly have enough capital to get the school started."

"I'll dig up everything I can on McDaniels as soon as we get back."

"When you do, I'd like to call him personally."

"You're the boss."

"Yeah, right. So you keep telling me."

We both laughed at that one, knowing that without each other this dream of mine would never have come true. Tracy was just as much a reason for its phenomenal success as I was.

Several days later, Tracy came by the house and told me everything she'd uncovered about Clay McDaniels.

"You missed your calling, girlfriend. You should have been a private investigator."

She laughed. "Hey, that's why you pay me the big bucks."

"How did you get all this information?"

"Computers are a wonderful thing, my dear. That and word of mouth. From reliable sources, of course."

I shook my head in amazement. We had information on him dating back to when he worked as a mailman in the Wall Street district, straight through his rise to owning his bonded courier service. According to Tracy's information, some of the most influential people in the world were his regular clients. The only thing missing in her dossier of information was anything personal.

"Does he have a life outside of his business?" I asked, my curiosity piqued.

"That's the only hole. There's not one word anywhere about family, friends. No gossip about women. Nothing. It's almost as if he lives and breathes work."

"That's odd, don't you think?"

She was quiet for a moment. "Is it? Are you any different? All your time and energy are devoted to your job. This cause is your life."

"That's different. I have my reasons. You know that. What kind of personal…life could I possibly hope to have?"

"You'll never know unless you give yourself a chance, Deanna. You've found your comfort zone again. Somewhere safe. Just like when you hid behind your music, then behind Cord, the hospital, the center, and now the Foundation."

"That's not true."

"Of course it is. That's not to say that you haven't done wonderful, incredible things, but you've never. allowed yourself to live. You've always given yourself up to something, or someone. When is it going to be Deanna's time?"

Later, I thought about what Tracy said, considered the veracity of her words. And I knew they were true, as hard as it was for me to admit. I was still afraid. With all that I had, all that I'd done, had endured and accomplished. I was still afraid. Scared witless to let my guard down, accept myself for who I was, and the hell with what others thought.

Maybe one day.

That day arrived when Clay McDaniels stood on my doorstep and I heard his voice, which seemed to magically fill all the empty spaces in my soul. I knew then that I wanted to take the chance.

I can't say exactly when our relationship shifted from *strictly business* to personal. To a relationship that dreams are made of. It was probably a lot of little things along the way, the walks to the ice-cream store, the intimate dinners we share, our first date at the South Street Seaport, or maybe it was when he confided in me about his failed marriage and the pain he felt from missing his son, or when I finally broke down and told him about Cord. But thinking about it now, it was all those things and more. The gentleness, the genuine caring, the laughter, and most of all the trust. So when we made love for the very first time, it was meant to be.

"I want to take care of you. Open the world to you through my eyes. I want to be the one you turn to," he whispered just before he took me in his arms and kissed me. In that instant I knew that I'd truly found love for the very first time in my life.

Making love with Clay was something that can't be described in words. He took me to a place I'd never been and cherished me, made my body feel it was truly a treasure. He made me feel and experience pleasure that had been denied me for so long.

When Clay vowed to me, as we lay curled in each others' arms, that each time would only get better, I believed him. Finally I believed that this thing called making love could get better, and that I was worthy of all the wonderful sensations I was feeling.

The first big thing of our blooming love relationship came much sooner than either of us would have anticipated. Not only would it test our love, but also whether or not I could be the woman Clay would need in his life.

CHAPTER XXII

"Dee, it's me, Clay."

My heart jumped. I could tell something was wrong. I clutched the phone a little tighter. "What is it? Is Matthew all right?"

He pushed out a breath. "Matt's fine. I'm the one who's a mess. His mother never came back to pick him up."

"What?"

"She just didn't show up. She planned it. She left a note in his bag."

"What did it say?"

"Basically that since her husband Steven walked out on her, she didn't feel she could manage to take care of Matt and knew that he'd be better off with me."

"Did she leave a number? Where is she?"

"No. And I have no idea where she is. The note said she'd mail his things once she got settled."

"But...what about Matt? The poor baby."

"Apparently she talked to him about it. He seems okay, but there's no way he can't be feeling abandoned. God, Dee, I don't know what to do. He needs to be in school. I have to arrange for child care...I don't know where to start."

"Why don't the two of you come over here? It would give me a chance to meet Matthew, and you and I can talk. We'll figure something out."

"I don't want to put this on you, Deanna. I mean, we just got our lives together. I can't expect you to take on my son as well."

My heart filled. Even with all that he suddenly had on his plate, he was still thinking of me. "Why don't you let me worry about that? You two come by about lunchtime." Where I was getting the courage from was a mystery to me, but it felt good.

I dashed around the house making sure that everything was perfect. I'd prepared sandwiches, a fruit salad, iced tea, and I had plenty of ice cream. Thinking that I had everything taken care of, I suddenly became a ball of nerves. What did I know about children? What made me think I could even begin to help Clay with his dilemma? What if Matthew hated me on sight?

The doorbell rang, and I nearly knocked the bowl of fruit off the counter. I took a deep breath and went to the door.

"Who is it?"

"It's Clay."

"And Matthew," a little voice chimed, and my chest tightened.

I opened the door, but did something I hadn't done in ages. I put on my dark glasses.

"Hi, come on in."

"Deanna, this is my son, Matthew McDaniels. Matthew, this is Ms. Winters. Say hello."

"Hi. I'm four."

I broke out in a grin. He had the cutest voice. A cross between Michael Bolton and Janet Jackson, raspy and sweet. "So I heard. That's pretty old. Do you go to school?"

"Yep, 'cause I'm smart."

"You keep it up, and you'll be a successful businessman like your daddy."

"I want to be Spiderman. See?"

He pushed something hard into my hand. A plastic toy. I rubbed my fingers across the surface, conjuring up an image of the comic-strip-turned-cartoon character. I felt Clay move closer to me, ready to come to the rescue.

"He's great. But I like Barbie." I handed the toy back.

"Yuck, that's for girls." I felt him move past me into the living room.

Clay squeezed my hand and brushed his lips against my cheek. "Think you can handle us for a whole afternoon?"

"Piece of cake," I said, and wondered again where this burgeoning sense of adventure had arisen. Wherever, I liked this newfound feeling of assertiveness.

I spread out an old blanket, and Clay helped me pack up the lunch I'd made into a huge wicker basket. We had a picnic lunch right on the living room floor.

"This is the perfect picnic," Clay said, biting into a tuna sandwich. "We don't have to worry about fighting for space on the grass, or fighting the bugs."

"I like bugs," Matt said.

Clay and I laughed.

"He can go out in the back if you want, Clay."

"Are you sure it's all right?"

"It's fenced in. If we sit in the kitchen, you can keep an eye on him from the window."

"Wanna go out in the yard, son?"

"Yeah!"

"I'll be right back." Clay got up and took Matthew into the yard. I started putting away our picnic fixings.

"I think he likes you." Clay eased up behind me to nibble on my ear. "But what red-blooded male wouldn't?"

I turned into his embrace, reaching up to capture the feel of his face with my hands. I rediscovered the cleft in his chin, the slope of his eyes, the sweeping silkiness of his brows. My thumb found his lips, which were full, inviting, and moist, seeming to send signals of imminent fulfillment. Oh, yes, I knew what those lips were capable of doing.

His hands glided down my sides. His fingers spread, finding all the secret, sensitive spots. A quick, hot chasm of want opened up inside of me, rushing like a wave of tropical heat to my center. I couldn't hold back the cry that surged out of me with the sudden force of arousal that hit me with the intensity of nature unleashed. He pulled me closer, tighter, belly to belly, chest to breasts. His mouth on mine was soft but demanding, moist and giving. His tongue sought entry into my mouth, and I yielded to the sweet nectar as his tongue dueled gingerly with mine, delving inside, once, twice, exploring, retreating.

I felt my knees turn weak, that hot spot between my thighs throbbed and grew moist, my nipples grew tight, erect. *This* was desire, this feeling of need that took hold of you and stole your breath away. It was a delirious sensation that I didn't want ever to stop.

"Dee. Can it always be like this?" he whispered against my mouth, nibbling on my bottom lip. "I don't know what's happening to me. I just know that I want you. Now. Always."

A mixture of emotions tumbled through me. What could I offer this man, and now his son? Would there come a time when he felt that I was inadequate? Would he come to resent my handicap and merely feel obliged to be with me?

I'd never know the answer if I wasn't willing to take the risk.

"It can be whatever we make it, Clay. And whatever is happening to you, is happening to me."

He kissed me again, sweet and gentle this time, sealing the unspoken promise.

And I knew I was in love.

We talked and laughed for hours while Matthew played in the yard, darting in and out of the house, because according to him, he was "dying of thirst."

"He's wonderful, Clay."

"Yeah, I think so, too."

I heard the pride and the anxiety in his voice. It was one thing to long for your child from afar, it was entirely different matter when what you thought and said you wanted all along is suddenly thrust at you. I knew. Not from a parent's perspective, but from a child's. Whenever my parents were forced to deal with my issues, they found another session for me to join, a new boarding school for me to attend, an additional instructor to sharpen my skills. I wouldn't want that for anyone's child. Clay had to find a way to make it right for both of them, or his son would grow up to resent him and his mother.

"Clay...until you get Matt registered in school...I'd like for him to stay here with me during the day, when you're working."

"Dee." He took my hand. "I couldn't ask you to do something like that."

"You didn't. I offered. And it's something I want to do."

"But—"

"If Matthew agrees, will you?"

He hesitated a moment. "Deal."

I let out a silent sigh of relief and smiled, secretly wondering what I'd gotten myself into.

The first week was difficult and challenging. As luck would have it, Clay had to be out of town for two weeks on a San Diego business trip that couldn't be rescheduled. He hadn't had time to find a school, and Matt's mother had yet to send necessities, like a birth certificate or immunization records. Without them, there was little we could do, except make the transition for Matthew as smooth as possible.

The days were easy. We ate breakfast together, and I learned that his favorite food was waffles, drenched in syrup. He played with his toys, watched *Sesame Street*, and ran around in the yard until lunchtime. I even began to give him piano lessons and found that he was a natural. He loved it and tried to play on his own whenever I was busy. Tracy usually stopped by for dinner and brought anything we needed from the store. It was the nights that were hard.

The first night he wanted me to read him a story. I got my first dose of reality.

"I wish I could, sweetheart," I said, sitting on the edge of the bed. "But I can't see the words."

"Why?"

"I was in an accident and I...can't see."

He was quiet for minute as if he was trying to make sense of what I said. "How do you know how to cook and put on your clothes? How come you don't fall down?"

I smiled. He wasn't put off, but curious. Slowly and simply as I could I explained to him how I managed my life without being able to see.

"If you take off your glasses, will you be able to see?"

"No. I won't."

"Oh." He settled back against the pillow. "Can you *tell* me a story?"

My throat tightened with emotion. "Sure," I whispered. I leaned back against the headrest and put an arm around him. He cuddled up next to me like we'd done this all our lives, and I felt my heart shift in my chest. Swallowing back the lump in my throat, I told him the story of a wonderful little boy and a magic horse named Dreammaker. And I had the satisfaction of holding a wonderful little boy as he slept in my arms.

Clay called every morning and every night during his absence, needing to be constantly assured that we were all right and that Matthew was just adjusting. He was tickled that his son had a talent for music, and Matt even played a short time for his father over the phone.

"Deanna, I can't thank you enough. I don't know what I would have done without your help."

"I'm enjoying every minute, Clay. Believe me. I suppose you never know what you're capable of doing until you've been put to the test."

"I love you, Deanna." It was almost a whisper, like a gentle breeze that barely ruffles your hair, soft but present.

Though in my heart I had known those were his feeling, he had never said the words until then. No man, not even my father, had ever said, *I love you, Deanna*.

Tears of joy welled in my eyes. I felt their heat on my cheeks, tasted their saltiness on my lips. My heart seemed to swell in my chest. I wanted to say something. Tell him I felt the same way, that I had for a long time and always would. But I couldn't speak, and I think he understood.

"Good night, sweetheart. Rest well. I'll see you both tomorrow."

Slowly I hung up the phone, holding onto the receiver as if I could somehow, magically, hold onto the words that had come through it. "I love you, too, Clay," I whispered. "And I love your son."

Perhaps my silent prayers had been answered, and God had, in fact, given me my child. I could only hope.

CHAPTER XXIII

Shortly after Clay's return from San Diego, two huge boxes with Matthew's belongings arrived at his house. Although I was happy that Clay had his son and that Matthew appeared to be adjusting to his new living arrangements, I couldn't help but wonder what kind of woman Rachael was. How could she have given up this wonderful treasure, this joy, even if it was to his own father? I'd only known Matt for a month, and already I knew that it would kill me to let him go. My greatest fear was that one day she'd suddenly materialize and take him away. Clay worried too.

"I'm going to seek legal custody of Matthew," he confided to me one evening when Matthew was out of earshot and absorbed with his Nintendo game.

"I was hoping that you would. I'm sure Tracy would be happy to work out the details for you. Get the paperwork rolling."

"Thanks, but I have an attorney. I don't want to pull Tracy into something that could turn ugly somewhere down the line. Rachael may turn up, and she may not."

"Have you heard anything else from her since the boxes arrived?"

"Not a word. And it's just as well. Anyway, I don't want to talk about Rachael. It gives me a headache." He leaned closer. I could feel his breath, with a hint of tomato sauce, brush across my face. "What I do want to talk about is a benefit dinner that's being given at the White House."

"You need me to keep Matthew while you're gone?"

"Actually, I wanted you to come with me."

"What?" My stomach seesawed.

"Yes, I want you to come with me. It'll be wonderful. We can spend a couple of days together." He nibbled my ear. "Folks need to see you, Dee. They've heard all these wonderful things you're doing at the Foundation, and still some believe in the rumors that you're just a phantom." His mouth against my temple was warm. Persuasive. "It will do you good. Since we started working together, you've stopped traveling completely."

"That was the whole point," I said, a bit more harshly than I intended. "I'm sorry," I stroked his cheek. "I didn't mean to snap at you, it's just…I guess I've grown comfortable again. I didn't want to rock the boat."

"Baby, I want you there with me, but the decision is yours. Whatever you decide is fine with me." He rose. "I'll tear Matt away from the Nintendo and get him to bed."

Since Matthew had come into our lives, he and his father practically moved in. And I loved it. I was getting to be the mother I never thought I could be.

Thinking about Clay's request, I started piling the dishes in the dishwasher. He was right. I did need to get out, move around in the world. Maybe I would go. I smiled, listening to the sounds of laughter coming from father and son. At least now, I had so much more to come home to.

Tracy was almost too happy to play auntie for the weekend. I gave her more instructions about Matthew than I'd ever given her for the distribution of millions of dollars. And for all his posturing, Clay was no better. You'd think we were going out of the country for a month.

"I'm about sick of you, girl." Tracy said, after I'd gone over Matt's breakfast, lunch, and bedtime routine for the *n*th time. "And Clay, if you don't back off, you're really going to get it. The whole weekend will be over by the time you two pains in the neck stop telling me what I need to do."

"Paul will take you guys anywhere you need to go," I added—referring to the chauffeur Cord had insisted I employ shortly after my accident—risking Tracy's wrath by mentioning that fact once again.

"Get out. Just get out!"

"Okay, okay, we're going," Clay mumbled. "Is it all right with you, *sergeant*, if we say goodbye to Matthew?"

"Five minutes."

"Gee, thanks," I said. We walked into the living room and found him in his favorite spot, at the piano.

After a near-tearful goodbye, we were finally on our way.

To say I was a nervous wreck entering the White House was an understatement. But it was a good kind of nervous. I could feel the energy, the glitter, the beauty. Voices in a multitude of accents floated around me, music, soft and soothing, glided like a spring breeze around the room. I may not be able to see, but the rest of my sense were sharply honed and created the pictures, the scents, and the atmosphere that would get me through the evening. I needed this, I realized, as Clay and I were introduced to one bigwig after another. I needed to be out in circulation again, practicing my *art* of seeing, testing my abilities, keeping them sharp. I know I would have never done something like this on my own, but with Clay at my side, I felt secure. Safe.

We were halfway through the evening when I felt Clay grow tense beside me. I was just about to ask him what was wrong, when he introduced me to Dr. Marcus Chandler, the man who believed he'd found a solution to my blindness. Although they were cordial, the friction between them was as thick as a London fog. It wasn't until much later that I understood why.

Marcus and I talked briefly about his work and the progress he'd made. A part of me was intrigued by the possibilities, another part was wary. I promised to talk with him more when I returned to New York.

"What is it that you have against Marcus?" I asked Clay several weeks after our dinner party welcoming Marcus to town.

"I don't have anything against him."

"Clay, I think I know you well enough to know when you're lying."

"I don't trust him," he snapped.

"Why? Because he's offering something revolutionary, or that he's offering it to me?"

Seconds of silence ticked away. Clay got out of bed and began to move restlessly around the room.

"Are we going to talk about this, Clay? I don't want whatever this is you're feeling to get between us."

"I don't know how to explain this to you, Deanna. It's more than just the procedure or its possibilities. Chandler wants more than that."

"Of course he does. Marcus Chandler is a driven man, just as you are. He sees his dream right at his fingertips, and he wants it."

"That's not what I mean."

"Then what do you mean?"

"He wants *you*, Deanna. You. It's obvious in the way he looks at you, from the moment he saw you."

He was jealous. Wow. I wanted to laugh, not because I thought it was funny, but because I thought it was great. In either case, I knew better. I eased out of bed and found him in the darkness of my bedroom, slipping my arms around his bare waist.

"Do you really think it matters what Marcus wants? What about what I want?"

He pulled me to him, brushing his face against my hair. I felt his heart thudding against my cheek.

"What do you want, Dee?"

"You, Matthew, the life we've begun building together. I want the Foundation and the Institute to help millions of kids. And if Marcus's procedure can accomplish that, I want that, too."

I dared not tell him of Marcus's confession of his feelings toward me, his devastation over his wife's death and how I filled that gap for him. Some things are better left unsaid.

"What if you...get your sight back, Dee?"

"What are you really asking me?"

He sighed heavily and turned away as if that would hide what was raging in his heart. "I'm scared, Dee. Scared that if—when you can see again—you won't need me anymore."

"Oh, Clay, you can't believe that. You think the only reason I need you is because I'm blind?" I was almost angry. In fact, I was angry. Angry that he could think so little of me. "I need you because of who you are. Because of what you've given to me, how you've enriched my life. And I would think, hope, that the same holds true for you."

"Deanna, I—" He suddenly gathered me in his arms, hugging me tight. "I just don't know what I'd do if I lost you. It's been so long since I've been really needed, wanted by someone I care so deeply about. And now there's Matthew, and you've been incredible with him. Everything is finally coming together. I know I can't be your whole world, Deanna. At least the rational part of me does. But I want to be as much of it as you'll let me. For as long as you'll let me."

"I don't have any reason to go anywhere, Clay." I touched his lips with mine. "I think I've finally found my place in the world too. And I'm liking it. As for Marcus, the operation, the risk...I really don't know. It's something I'll have to give careful thought to, Clay. And it's a decision that only I can make."

It was a decision I'd battled with for two weeks, right up to this moment, right here, right now, tonight at Radio City Music Hall. But as the emcee called my name and the audience rose to their feet, I knew that there was really no doubt in my mind what I wanted.

CHAPTER XXIV

Deanna Winters stood in front of the microphone, and after what seemed like an eternity, the crowd finally quieted and resumed their seats.

"Thank you all so much. For everything. Your thoughts, your prayers, and your support," Deanna began in that melodic voice that had the power to mesmerize. "This Humanitarian Award means more to me than words can convey. I know it is to symbolize the wonderful things that a person does in their lifetime. But the award is not mine alone. It is yours, too. the Deanna Winters Foundation and the Institute would not be possible without all of you. I am honored to be a part of a dream-turned-into-reality for so many. Children around the world have been the recipients of your kindness, your contributions.

"There are so many I want to thank who have been instrumental in making this day a possibility. First and foremost God, who although He gives, He takes away. Yet, even in that, He replaces. When I lost my sight, I believed I had been forsaken, punished. It took finding a purpose in life, a goal, to help me realize that what appeared to be a tragedy was actually a blessing. Through my injury, I was able to gain more than what I believed I lost. I gained a sense of myself and all that I was capable of doing, of giving.

"I want to thank my dear sister-friend Tracy Moore, who has been instrumental in helping me keep my sanity and run the organizations. She has been through all my triumphs, my failures, and my tantrums and she still remained my friend, my sister." She felt her eyes missing over, and, knowing Tracy, she was boo-hooing. But Deanna refused to cry.

She took a steady breath. "I want to thank Cord Herrera. Many things were and will be said about Cord throughout his life and his career. But what has never been said, what the tabloids and gossips have never mentioned, was that he was one of the reasons that forced me to go on, to take a look at myself and take a stand against the odds. For that, Cord, I will always be in your debt."

A tumultuous round of applause filled the auditorium, and the spotlight sought out and found him. An image of his face filled the screen, and the whole world saw Cord Herrera as they'd never seen him before. Humbled.

Cord bowed his head. He didn't need to tell Deanna that he had loved her in his own way. Somehow she always knew.

"And thank you to a true champion, Dr. St. Claire, who tirelessly instilled in me the ability to believe in myself, that I could see without sight. Thank you. I'd also like to thank Dr. Marcus Chandler, a man with courage and a vision. A man who offered me the chance of a lifetime. The chance to see again."

A rush of whispers permeated the audience. Heads everywhere turned looking for this miracle worker.

"But I finally realized that my sight wasn't what made me who I am, rather the lack of it did. I know that your work will change the course of many lives, Dr. Chandler. I know it changed mine."

Hidden in the crowd, Marcus accepted her decision, finally understanding what she had been trying to say to him for months. Now, he too, could move on. But he'd never forget Deanna or the impact she had on his life.

"And finally, I want to thank Clay McDaniels, the real miracle in my life. The man of my dreams come true. The unconditional support, love, and kindness I received from you should be experienced by everyone at least once in a lifetime. Thank you, Clay, for coming into my life and bringing Matthew with you. I love you."

As the audience applauded, Clay felt as if a tidal wave were rushing through him. His insides filled, his eyes clouded over, and yes, he cried. In front of the whole world, he cried. She'd finally said, in front of billions, the words he'd longed to hear. She declared her love for him in front of the world. *His Deanna.* Finally.

"Thank you, everyone," Deanna said. "I'll treasure this moment, this award, this night, forever."

EPILOGUE

The sounds of clapping, the shouting of her name, the sparks of flashbulbs receded as Paul hustled Clay and Deanna away from the night's extravaganza and toward their sanctuary.

Clay put his arm around Deanna and hugged her close, placing a gentle kiss on her forehead. "You were incredible tonight. I can't describe it. You held everyone in the palm of your hand, including me."

She turned into his embrace, resting her head on his chest, thinking about the turns in her life which led to tonight. She was happy. Truly happy with the way things were, how she was. Yes, she was happy.

"Are you sure about the operation?" he asked. "I don't want you to refuse it because of anything I may have said."

She put her finger to his lips. "Sssh. One thing I discovered that was more important than any other lesson...I don't need my sight to feel love, to see inside your heart, or to know what's in mine. I'm well, better than I've ever been, and life can only get better as long as you're in it with me. You've been my quiet storm, Clay. Always on the horizon. Steady enough to ruffle my feathers, strong enough to withstand my doubts, cleansing enough to wash away past hurts. And you brought me sunshine."

She stroked his face, visualizing the planes, the soft and rough spots, the slope of his eyes, the fullness of his lips.

"I love you, my darling Deanna."

"And I love you."

Their mouths met, joined, explored, sealed what was in their hearts. And in that moment she truly saw the brightness of her future.

ABOUT THE AUTHOR

Donna Hill's first romance was published in 1990. From there it was an array of writing successes which have garnered her countless devoted fans. Her business, health and relationship articles have appeared in newspapers and magazines across the country. She has been featured in *Essence, Black Enterprise* and *New York Newsday*, among others. Donna has had fourteen books published to date and is busy at work on her seventeenth title. She is currently a publicist for the Queens Borough Public Library system, the largest public library in the country. She lives in Brooklyn, New York, with her family.

2007 Publication Schedule

January

Rooms of the Heart
Donna Hill
ISBN-13: 978-1-58571-219-9
ISBN-10: 1-58571-219-1
$6.99

A Dangerous Love
J. M. Jeffries
ISBN-13: 978-1-58571-217-5
ISBN-10: 1-58571-217-5
$6.99

February

Bound By Love
Beverly Clark
ISBN-13: 978-1-58571-232-8
ISBN-10: 1-58571-232-9
$6.99

A Love to Cherish
Beverly Clark
ISBN-13: 978-1-58571-233-5
ISBN-10: 1-58571-233-7
$6.99

March

Best of Friends
Natalie Dunbar
ISBN-13: 978-1-58571-220-5
ISBN-10: 1-58571-220-5
$6.99

Midnight Magic
Gwynne Forster
ISBN-13: 978-1-58571-225-0
ISBN-10: 1-58571-225-6
$6.99

April

Cherish the Flame
Beverly Clark
ISBN-13: 978-1-58571-221-2
ISBN-10: 1-58571-221-3
$6.99

Quiet Storm
Donna Hill
ISBN-13: 978-1-58571-226-7
ISBN-10: 1-58571-226-4
$6.99

May

Sweet Tomorrows
Kimberley White
ISBN-13: 978-1-58571-234-2
ISBN-10: 1-58571-234-5
$6.99

No Commitment Required
Seressia Glass
ISBN-13: 978-1-58571-222-9
ISBN-10: 1-58571-222-1
$6.99

June

A Dangerous Deception
J. M. Jeffries
ISBN-13: 978-1-58571-228-1
ISBN-10: 1-58571-228-0
$6.99

Illusions
Pamela Leigh Starr
ISBN-13: 978-1-58571-229-8
ISBN-10: 1-58571-229-9
$6.99

2007 Publication Schedule (continued)

July

Indiscretions
Donna Hill
ISBN-13: 978-1-58571-230-4
ISBN-10: 1-58571-230-2
$6.99

Whispers in the Night
Dorothy Elizabeth Love
ISBN-13: 978-1-58571-231-1
ISBN-10: 1-58571-231-1
$6.99

August

Bodyguard
Andrea Jackson
ISBN-13: 978-1-58571-235-9
ISBN-10: 1-58571-235-3
$6.99

Crossing Paths, Tempting Memories
Dorothy Elizabeth Love
ISBN-13: 978-1-58571-236-6
ISBN-10: 1-58571-236-1
$6.99

September

Fate
Pamela Leigh Starr
ISBN-13: 978-1-58571-258-8
ISBN-10: 1-58571-258-2
$6.99

Mae's Promise
Melody Walcott
ISBN-13: 978-1-58571-259-5
ISBN-10: 1-58571-259-0
$6.99

October

Magnolia Sunset
Giselle Carmichael
ISBN-13: 978-1-58571-260-1
ISBN-10: 1-58571-260-4
$6.99

Broken
Dar Tomlinson
ISBN-13: 978-1-58571-261-8
ISBN-10: 1-58571-261-2
$6.99

November

Truly Inseparable
Wanda Y. Thomas
ISBN-13: 978-1-58571-262-5
ISBN-10: 1-58571-262-0
$6.99

The Color Line
Lizzette G. Carter
ISBN-13: 978-1-58571-263-2
ISBN-10: 1-58571-263-9
$6.99

December

Love Always
Mildred Riley
ISBN-13: 978-1-58571-264-9
ISBN-10: 1-58571-264-7
$6.99

Pride and Joi
Gay Gunn
ISBN-13: 978-1-58571-265-6
ISBN-10: 1-58571-265-5
$6.99

Other Genesis Press, Inc. Titles

A Dangerous Deception	J.M. Jeffries	$8.95
A Dangerous Love	J.M. Jeffries	$8.95
A Dangerous Obsession	J.M. Jeffries	$8.95
A Drummer's Beat to Mend	Kei Swanson	$9.95
A Happy Life	Charlotte Harris	$9.95
A Heart's Awakening	Veronica Parker	$9.95
A Lark on the Wing	Phyliss Hamilton	$9.95
A Love of Her Own	Cheris F. Hodges	$9.95
A Love to Cherish	Beverly Clark	$8.95
A Risk of Rain	Dar Tomlinson	$8.95
A Twist of Fate	Beverly Clark	$8.95
A Will to Love	Angie Daniels	$9.95
Acquisitions	Kimberley White	$8.95
Across	Carol Payne	$12.95
After the Vows	Leslie Esdaile	$10.95
(Summer Anthology)	T.T. Henderson	
	Jacqueline Thomas	
Again My Love	Kayla Perrin	$10.95
Against the Wind	Gwynne Forster	$8.95
All I Ask	Barbara Keaton	$8.95
Ambrosia	T.T. Henderson	$8.95
An Unfinished Love Affair	Barbara Keaton	$8.95
And Then Came You	Dorothy Elizabeth Love	$8.95
Angel's Paradise	Janice Angelique	$9.95
At Last	Lisa G. Riley	$8.95
Best of Friends	Natalie Dunbar	$8.95
Beyond the Rapture	Beverly Clark	$9.95
Blaze	Barbara Keaton	$9.95
Blood Lust	J. M. Jeffries	$9.95
Bodyguard	Andrea Jackson	$9.95
Boss of Me	Diana Nyad	$8.95
Bound by Love	Beverly Clark	$8.95

Other Genesis Press, Inc. Titles (continued)

Breeze	Robin Hampton Allen	$10.95
Broken	Dar Tomlinson	$24.95
By Design	Barbara Keaton	$8.95
Cajun Heat	Charlene Berry	$8.95
Careless Whispers	Rochelle Alers	$8.95
Cats & Other Tales	Marilyn Wagner	$8.95
Caught in a Trap	Andre Michelle	$8.95
Caught Up In the Rapture	Lisa G. Riley	$9.95
Cautious Heart	Cheris F Hodges	$8.95
Chances	Pamela Leigh Starr	$8.95
Cherish the Flame	Beverly Clark	$8.95
Class Reunion	Irma Jenkins/	
	John Brown	$12.95
Code Name: Diva	J.M. Jeffries	$9.95
Conquering Dr. Wexler's Heart	Kimberley White	$9.95
Crossing Paths,	Dorothy Elizabeth Love	$9.95
Tempting Memories		
Cypress Whisperings	Phyllis Hamilton	$8.95
Dark Embrace	Crystal Wilson Harris	$8.95
Dark Storm Rising	Chinelu Moore	$10.95
Daughter of the Wind	Joan Xian	$8.95
Deadly Sacrifice	Jack Kean	$22.95
Designer Passion	Dar Tomlinson	$8.95
Dreamtective	Liz Swados	$5.95
Ebony Butterfly II	Delilah Dawson	$14.95
Echoes of Yesterday	Beverly Clark	$9.95
Eden's Garden	Elizabeth Rose	$8.95
Everlastin' Love	Gay G. Gunn	$8.95
Everlasting Moments	Dorothy Elizabeth Love	$8.95
Everything and More	Sinclair Lebeau	$8.95
Everything but Love	Natalie Dunbar	$8.95
Eve's Prescription	Edwina Martin Arnold	$8.95

Other Genesis Press, Inc. Titles (continued)

Falling	Natalie Dunbar	$9.95
Fate	Pamela Leigh Starr	$8.95
Finding Isabella	A.J. Garrotto	$8.95
Forbidden Quest	Dar Tomlinson	$10.95
Forever Love	Wanda Y. Thomas	$8.95
From the Ashes	Kathleen Suzanne	$8.95
	Jeanne Sumerix	
Gentle Yearning	Rochelle Alers	$10.95
Glory of Love	Sinclair LeBeau	$10.95
Go Gentle into that Good Night	Malcom Boyd	$12.95
Goldengroove	Mary Beth Craft	$16.95
Groove, Bang, and Jive	Steve Cannon	$8.99
Hand in Glove	Andrea Jackson	$9.95
Hard to Love	Kimberley White	$9.95
Hart & Soul	Angie Daniels	$8.95
Heartbeat	Stephanie Bedwell-Grime	$8.95
Hearts Remember	M. Loui Quezada	$8.95
Hidden Memories	Robin Allen	$10.95
Higher Ground	Leah Latimer	$19.95
Hitler, the War, and the Pope	Ronald Rychiak	$26.95
How to Write a Romance	Kathryn Falk	$18.95
I Married a Reclining Chair	Lisa M. Fuhs	$8.95
Indigo After Dark Vol. I	Nia Dixon/Angelique	$10.95
Indigo After Dark Vol. II	Dolores Bundy/	$10.95
	Cole Riley	
Indigo After Dark Vol. III	Montana Blue/	$10.95
	Coco Morena	
Indigo After Dark Vol. IV	Cassandra Colt/	$14.95
	Diana Richeaux	
Indigo After Dark Vol. V	Delilah Dawson	$14.95
Icie	Pamela Leigh Starr	$8.95
I'll Be Your Shelter	Giselle Carmichael	$8.95

Other Genesis Press, Inc. Titles (continued)

I'll Paint a Sun	A.J. Garrotto	$9.95
Illusions	Pamela Leigh Starr	$8.95
Indiscretions	Donna Hill	$8.95
Intentional Mistakes	Michele Sudler	$9.95
Interlude	Donna Hill	$8.95
Intimate Intentions	Angie Daniels	$8.95
Jolie's Surrender	Edwina Martin-Arnold	$8.95
Kiss or Keep	Debra Phillips	$8.95
Lace	Giselle Carmichael	$9.95
Last Train to Memphis	Elsa Cook	$12.95
Lasting Valor	Ken Olsen	$24.95
Let Us Prey	Hunter Lundy	$25.95
Life Is Never As It Seems	J.J. Michael	$12.95
Lighter Shade of Brown	Vicki Andrews	$8.95
Love Always	Mildred E. Riley	$10.95
Love Doesn't Come Easy	Charlyne Dickerson	$8.95
Love Unveiled	Gloria Greene	$10.95
Love's Deception	Charlene Berry	$10.95
Love's Destiny	M. Loui Quezada	$8.95
Mae's Promise	Melody Walcott	$8.95
Magnolia Sunset	Giselle Carmichael	$8.95
Matters of Life and Death	Lesego Malepe, Ph.D.	$15.95
Meant to Be	Jeanne Sumerix	$8.95
Midnight Clear	Leslie Esdaile	$10.95
(Anthology)	Gwynne Forster	
	Carmen Green	
	Monica Jackson	
Midnight Magic	Gwynne Forster	$8.95
Midnight Peril	Vicki Andrews	$10.95
Misconceptions	Pamela Leigh Starr	$9.95
Montgomery's Children	Richard Perry	$14.95
My Buffalo Soldier	Barbara B. K. Reeves	$8.95

Other Genesis Press, Inc. Titles (continued)

Naked Soul	Gwynne Forster	$8.95
Next to Last Chance	Louisa Dixon	$24.95
No Apologies	Seressia Glass	$8.95
No Commitment Required	Seressia Glass	$8.95
No Regrets	Mildred E. Riley	$8.95
Nowhere to Run	Gay G. Gunn	$10.95
O Bed! O Breakfast!	Rob Kuehnle	$14.95
Object of His Desire	A. C. Arthur	$8.95
Office Policy	A. C. Arthur	$9.95
Once in a Blue Moon	Dorianne Cole	$9.95
One Day at a Time	Bella McFarland	$8.95
Outside Chance	Louisa Dixon	$24.95
Passion	T.T. Henderson	$10.95
Passion's Blood	Cherif Fortin	$22.95
Passion's Journey	Wanda Y. Thomas	$8.95
Past Promises	Jahmel West	$8.95
Path of Fire	T.T. Henderson	$8.95
Path of Thorns	Annetta P. Lee	$9.95
Peace Be Still	Colette Haywood	$12.95
Picture Perfect	Reon Carter	$8.95
Playing for Keeps	Stephanie Salinas	$8.95
Pride & Joi	Gay G. Gunn	$15.95
Pride & Joi	Gay G. Gunn	$8.95
Promises to Keep	Alicia Wiggins	$8.95
Quiet Storm	Donna Hill	$10.95
Reckless Surrender	Rochelle Alers	$6.95
Red Polka Dot in a World of Plaid	Varian Johnson	$12.95
Reluctant Captive	Joyce Jackson	$8.95
Rendezvous with Fate	Jeanne Sumerix	$8.95
Revelations	Cheris F. Hodges	$8.95
Rivers of the Soul	Leslie Esdaile	$8.95

Other Genesis Press, Inc. Titles (continued)

Rocky Mountain Romance	Kathleen Suzanne	$8.95
Rooms of the Heart	Donna Hill	$8.95
Rough on Rats and Tough on Cats	Chris Parker	$12.95
Secret Library Vol. 1	Nina Sheridan	$18.95
Secret Library Vol. 2	Cassandra Colt	$8.95
Shades of Brown	Denise Becker	$8.95
Shades of Desire	Monica White	$8.95
Shadows in the Moonlight	Jeanne Sumerix	$8.95
Sin	Crystal Rhodes	$8.95
So Amazing	Sinclair LeBeau	$8.95
Somebody's Someone	Sinclair LeBeau	$8.95
Someone to Love	Alicia Wiggins	$8.95
Song in the Park	Martin Brant	$15.95
Soul Eyes	Wayne L. Wilson	$12.95
Soul to Soul	Donna Hill	$8.95
Southern Comfort	J.M. Jeffries	$8.95
Still the Storm	Sharon Robinson	$8.95
Still Waters Run Deep	Leslie Esdaile	$8.95
Stories to Excite You	Anna Forrest/Divine	$14.95
Subtle Secrets	Wanda Y. Thomas	$8.95
Suddenly You	Crystal Hubbard	$9.95
Sweet Repercussions	Kimberley White	$9.95
Sweet Tomorrows	Kimberly White	$8.95
Taken by You	Dorothy Elizabeth Love	$9.95
Tattooed Tears	T. T. Henderson	$8.95
The Color Line	Lizzette Grayson Carter	$9.95
The Color of Trouble	Dyanne Davis	$8.95
The Disappearance of Allison Jones	Kayla Perrin	$5.95
The Honey Dipper's Legacy	Pannell-Allen	$14.95
The Joker's Love Tune	Sidney Rickman	$15.95

Other Genesis Press, Inc. Titles (continued)

Order Form

Mail to: Genesis Press, Inc.
P.O. Box 101
Columbus, MS 39703

Name _____
Address _____
City/State _____ Zip _____
Telephone _____

Ship to (if different from above)
Name _____
Address _____
City/State _____ Zip _____
Telephone _____

Credit Card Information
Credit Card # _____ ☐ Visa ☐ Mastercard
Expiration Date (mm/yy) _____ ☐ AmEx ☐ Discover

Qty.	Author	Title	Price	Total

Use this order form, or call 1-888-INDIGO-1	
Total for books	
Shipping and handling: $5 first two books, $1 each additional book	
Total S & H	
Total amount enclosed	

Mississippi residents add 7% sales tax